Murder and Mayhem at Rosewood Hall

by Marilyn Valentine

This is a work of fiction. Names, characters, places, and incidents either are the product of the author's imagination or are used fictitiously. Any resemblance to actual persons, living or dead, events, or locales is entirely coincidental.

Copyright © 2021 by Marilyn Valentine

All rights reserved.

All rights reserved. No part of this book may be reproduced or used in any manner without written permission of the copyright owner except for the use of quotations in a book review.

First paperback edition April 2021

ISBN 9798740437026 (paperback)

Also by Marilyn Valentine

Friends, Angels and Revenge

Chapter 1

Lady Charlotte Sherringham or Shelly as she was known to her close friends sat back in her favourite arm chair and sipped her tea. She had broken off her engagement and should have been feeling sad or upset but she really felt as though a huge weight had been lifted off of her shoulders, should one feel relieved at a moment like this? She thought possibly not. He was a very wealthy man and would have been the answer to most of her financial problems but she couldn't face spending the rest of her life as his wife or when she thought about it even a day. She would never be able to love him, he wanted her because of who she was, something to add to his collection and not for herself, he did not love her, did that even make sense, and why had she accepted him, now she knew she disliked him, well she had been numb and confused when he had asked her and she had accepted, it seemed not to matter nothing did, it was a way to let someone else take over so she would not have to think or feel, to save her home too, then later it felt so wrong. They did not see each other after he had put a diamond ring on her finger she was glad to say, until this morning, and then looking at him she had realized she could not go through with it and she had given him the ring back, he took it, gave her a stiff, cold little bow and left without another word. Oh dear she was in such a pickle. She had to find a different answer. She sighed she hadn't any training of any kind, until a year ago she had been her father's spoiled little girl, pampered, her every whim at her finger tips. A huge wardrobe filled with clothes, and her jewels he had lavished on her was not going to do a lot to save Rosewood Hall. A year ago a lifetime when everything changed on that dreadful day when her beloved father and brother Simon had been killed in that fatal car crash. They had both loved fast cars, the crash had hit the news, so many cards flowers and well wishers, the funeral, all the people, it had seemed like a nightmare and she had somehow wandered though it, she had not been able to wake from it or rather when she did it was to find herself in deep trouble as well as grief. They were buried in the family plot in the local churchyard, she often took flowers down from the gardens and asked them why they had left her? This was all hers now, her home Rosewood Hall she loved more than anything.

The house was a huge rambling place that some ancestor had built. A reward for helping a king a long long time ago. Her family had lived here ever since, the thought of losing it was unbearable, she had to find a way, one that did not mean marrying a man she disliked. Two tears had escaped and ran unchecked down her face, she put her face in her hands, and then she quickly dabbed the tears away, this will not do, crying will only make my eyes red, it will not solve anything, she had to save her home, she also was responsible for all the servants they had all been at the hall for as long as she could remember, this was their home too, nobody ever left. The new ones that came were all related to each other.

Just then Chalfont her butler came in he pretended not to notice that she had been crying.

" More tea My Lady?" he asked as if nothing had happened and her whole world was not falling apart.

" Yes Chalfont and please tell Mrs Barclay her scones were delicious as always."

"Very good My Lady she will be happy to hear it." It was a time honoured routine and one that fit comfortably, it was home, she felt better, she would fight for this she had lost too much already.

When Shelly had finished her tea she nodded her head she could not undo the past no matter how much she wanted to, her family like many others had lost much of their money over the centuries to taxes and hard times she had not known or even needed to worry about this before, her father had always taken care of everything for her and Simon, they had been given everything, her father had indulged himself too, they had travelled and been invited everywhere. She had been society's darling, she had dreamed about falling in love and marrying one day but sometime in the future with a vague figure, a distant dream, a hero to fall in love with, she had been so happy the way things were, oh why had it all gone to horribly wrong? She heard no answer, well she had to move on, do her duty, do her best to solve it all herself. No knight riding in wearing shining armour was coming to save her. She had stayed here where she was loved and cared for, avoided London , she could not bear the endless pitying looks, she was in mourning anyway.

    She had turned down offers of house visits. Shelly felt better left to roam about as she had always done so as a child in the grounds and woods where she felt free, she could almost believe her father and brother were still here, almost, but now it was time to wake up she had to live her life. Her father had been admired and also envied, she had heard the whispers, he had been reckless possibly drinking and driving too fast, but she knew her father better.. He did like a drink and always to enjoy himself with friends but he loved and respected his motor cars and he would never drink and drive and never ever would he do anything to put his beloved son and heir in danger. The hall would have been Simon's in the course of time but now it had come to her, her father's will had seen to that, they had no male relatives left anyway so it was all hers. Rosewood Hall was hers and she was determined to keep it. She loved every stone, it was filled with happy memories.

She knew one thing she could do, one of the things her father and brother had loved and shared was a collection of rare cars, there was a large garage, formally a coach house and stables that they had turned into a home for their much prized collection. She would sell them, Shelly had put it off as long as possible it would be another link to them and her past lost but it had to be done, she had no idea how to go about it but she knew somebody who would, somebody she could trust to do it all for her and save herself some more pain. When she had hidden herself away from the world to heal in the place she loved best she had kept in touch and spent time with only one of her old childhood friends and in fact Simon's best friend, Archie. He had not made a fuss, had given her a hanky when she needed one, held her, had walked in the woods with her and had tea, all the things they had done as children, he was her friend, he understood, and he was not as broke as she was, and she knew he would help her.

Shelly went to the phone after morning coffee the next day, she had made a lot of plans over night. She had not slept much but she felt more refreshed now she had a plan, at last she was going to act, fight back at fate, sort out a future. She had dressed with her maid's help carefully that morning, she had thrown off her mourning clothes at last and it seemed as though she had thrown off her lack of purpose with them. Shelly looked at the young woman in the mirror, she saw a pale faced sad looking girl with dark gold hair and tied back with a velvet band, and dark blue eyes, she was wearing a blue floral silk shirt and darker blue skirt, flat navy shoes and stockings. She had put on her gold chain necklace, earrings and bracelet, she shook her curls and straightened her back, her maid Polly said "You look much better

Lady Shelly, more like yourself again blue was always your colour."

They had both got used to everything black for so long.

"Thank you Polly, I do feel lighter somehow." She made her phone call.

Shelly got through to a London number and spoke to Potters. Archie's man, "Good morning Potters, please put me through to Archie."

"Good morning My Lady I will just see if Mr Lakeland is available."

" Tell him to get out of bed the day is almost over the lazy beast, I know he is there," she huffed.

" Very good My Lady," Potters sighed really these young things.

" What ho young Shelly what is the meaning of disturbing a chap in the middle of the night?"
Shelly snorted in a very unladylike way "It's daytime Archie. You should know I have broken off the engagement it would not have done, I could not go through with it, but never mind that now, I

have another better plan and I need your help."

Archie answered warily, although he had not really liked the engagement but he was not sure he wanted to get involved in a plan sounded like hard work and troublesome, Shelly and Simon had always been up to mischief and often dragged him into it.

" Err what plan is that old thing, always want to help and so on but I mean what plan?" he asked carefully.

"Come down for lunch, I will tell all then, oh and tell Potters to shove a few things in an overnight bag." With that she hung up without giving him time to make up an excuse, she knew him too well and treated like a brother.

" But Shelly old girl always ready to do my bit but" he had heard the phone click and stared at the piece in his hand, "Well if that wasn't just like a woman, tricky things women love them dearly of course but they get you every time."

" Quite so sir," said Potters He was pleased he and Chalfont. Got on well.

Archie sighed " Oh well you know the lady, better pack a bag do as she asks and find out what she is up to or it will end up as something worse."

" Very good sir."

"Oh and you are coming too, we will take the car. Potters nodded glumly maybe he would get to drive, at a nice steady pace he was not a fan of speed as his master was, he would look forward to staying the night at the hall with his old chum Chalfont though.

Archie was busy thinking as he dressed and got ready to drive down to the hall. He was really glad the engagement was off she would never have been happy with that cold fish Jeremy Coulter, he would have disapproved of everything she did when she stopped grieving and become her old self again he would not have understood her at all. He would have made her most unhappy. Archie had been very surprised when she had told him by phone of the engagement and then she had burst into tears, not a good sign when announcing and engagement, or like herself at all, but still that was understandable. still grieving an so on. What on earth had made her do such a thing, Jeremy had stepped in quick and caught her unawares , she was beautiful after all but Archie had wisely guessed her father's unique car collection had a lot to do with it, The Hall too was also a beautiful place very old of course but he had good memories of long holidays with his chums. The Hall had been a second home to him. He knew he would have lost that if she had married that bounder Jeremy that's one reason why Archie did not like him Also there something wrong about Coulter and he didn't know what also he saw Archie as a threat Archie knew.

    Archie had advised at the time "Don't do it old girl, not a good thing don't you know." She had made vague noises of agreement and told him she would break it off soon.
Yes he was very glad the engagement was off but wondered what she was about to drag him into next. He sighed and got ready

    While Archie was finishing getting ready Shelly had her own plans she rang for Chalfont..

    " Chalfont I need to talk to you"

    "As you wish My Lady" he said sadly misunderstanding her reason.

"We are in trouble and I have plan to save us, but I will need all of your help to do it, and Chalfont thank you for standing by me."

The butler gave a little bow "Always a pleasure Lady Shelly to serve you."

" Please ask all the staff to to attend a meeting in half an hour on the terrace and I will explain how we are going to do it, oh and tell Mrs Barclay Archie will be coming for lunch."

"Very good My Lady I will see to it, can I help in any other way?"

"I am hoping so, I will need your help to make this plan work Chalfont it is the only way, I have thought at lot about it. Archie will be staying and bringing Potters too."

"The rooms will be ready." Chalfont left Shelly to arrange matters, but he went with a lighter step, she was fighting back. At last.

Shelly sat back she looked across the terrace to the garden and sighed all this was hers and it was never meant to be, all the responsibilities, she was going to take a huge step into the unknown to keep it she felt a little scared and excited, but at last she felt something other than grief.

Chalfont gave a slight cough to get her attention, all the staff were lined up on the terrace in front of her

Mrs. Barclay the excellent cook was gripping the sides of her apron, the rest of the staff looked nervous too they all of course knew the position of things, death duties were crippling, and were wondering about their fate and future this was their home and they were happy here, they all knew this was the moment of truth , it was a moment they had all dreaded although they they had known it had to come sadly.

Chalfont had assembled them. Shelly smiled at all of them reassuringly.

"I know things had been strange since err since the deaths." Her voice wavered. She took a deep breath. "Well now it's time to work out a plan to build a new future for all of us. We are going to save Rosewood Hall."

Chalfont nodded "May I ask how to proceed to assist you?" Mrs. Barclay looked at Shelly "My Lady we are all prepared to take a cut in wages if that helps, we all want to do all we can to keep our places here. I grew up here my mother was housekeeper then and I have always been happy to serve the Sherringham family and I hope I have always given satisfaction."

Shelly was touched by this gesture and said so. Shelly blinked back a tear and said softly " Dear Barky there is no need for any of that kind of sacrifice or at least I hope not., I have a plan to save our home for all us that want to stay, I will of course understand and do all I can to help any of you who wish to leave."

The staff all looked at each other and gave a little nod at Chalfont. Old Williams the gardener said "I bain't leaving." Chalfont gave his little cough as his answer then spoke to Shelly.

"I believe I speak for all of us here when I say we all behind you."

Shelly gave a small gruff laugh "You may not be when you hear what I propose. I have thought about this very carefully and I can only find one solution. I hope you will stay with me as I am going to need you all and your expert advise to make this work.

Chapter 2

So here it is, the way to save our home is to share it, I mean to turn the Hall into a very select guest house, we will let rooms to only very carefully chosen guests. Times are changing and we have to move with them to survive. The old ways are gone a lot of our old friends are as poor as church mice, there are new wealthy people and they are the ones who would jump at the chance to live in a place like the hall, we can offer the chance to experience life in a country house like the hall, boating on the lake, fishing in our private part of the river, tennis, the park, woods in fact the kind of way of life they have only read about." She paused for breath and to let them digest this she knew that servants like those from a large house like the hall were snobs and were proud to work for the titled old families.

Chalfont had his head bowed and was listening intently. Shelly waited, her butler was the key to making this work and she needed him the most. He knew every inch of her home as she did and loved it but he knew how it all worked and how to run it. She did not.

The butler lifted his head and gave a tiny nod , his eyebrows twitched almost as if in a coded message to the rest of the staff. Shelly let out breath she didn't know until that moment that she was holding.

"I know it is not ideal but the alternative is worse."
Some of the staff looked shocked they had guessed things were bad , there had been talk when Chalfont was not within hearing range, some had been expecting to have to leave and were relieved not to do so, this was a good place and she was easy to work for not like some they had heard about. a lot of their friends envied them.

Chalfont spoke " I will do all I can to assist you My Lady, may I inquire how you plan to go ahead? I ask so we the staff know what we should do. You will have to choose carefully who you allow to stay in the hall."

" Thank you all of you, I hoped you would all stay and I wanted you to know first before I took my plans further. It will be like having guests to stay but for longer periods. Any who do not suit will be asked to leave, but I don't think it will come to that. They will be well chosen. The important and different thing will be they will be paying to stay here, horrid I know but necessary to keep the hall, some other friends are selling and moving abroad, I do not want to do that" she gave a little sigh.

Mrs. Barclay wanted to hug her such a brave little soul she was thinking. instead she said "We are all with you My Lady and will do what we can, I suggest we get some more girls, two should do it as laundry and chamber maids, will the guests bring their own linen, maids and so on?"

Shelley blinked and then laughed "Maids possibly so, we shall have to see, this is all new to me. That's the spirit though what would I do without you Barky? We must look at this as an adventure and also a new way of life. I am glad to listen to any suggestions."

" Set menus would be helpful of course like usual guests would have, using our own produce as much as possible" suggested Mrs Barclay.

Shelly answered "Yes I'll leave that part to you"

Chalfont looked at Shelly's bewilderment and gave a little cough to show this was at an end and a conversation for later and downstairs.

The staff all smiled thanked Shelly and left to go about their business talking loudly as they went and making plans and suggestions."

"I will bring you some tea at once My Lady."
Shelly smiled and said with a sigh of relief "Yes please and that went better than I hoped and thanks to you."

The butler gave a little bow, he had plans of his own and then in no time at all was back with her tea, he had known she would need it and had left it all ready to make for her.

Shelley sipped the tea gratefully that he poured for her.

" Any ideas or suggestions from you Chalfont? I rely on your wise council. Things will change but we will try to keep it as though they haven't. The sort of guests we take on will be wealthy and expect the old traditional way of things in a country house after all that is what they will be paying for."

"I agree My Lady, but we have to choose carefully, the hall has some very valuable things and yes we must keep standards high."

"We will Chalfont we will, I will check each one and require references of the highest, also some may come from word of mouth, and recommendations from friends. I shall keep the west wing my own, my room is already there so that will be easy to organize."

"We will need extra staff depending on how many guests we cater for."

"I think half a dozen to start with and see how we manage, it well give the right impression too and we will be charging high prices for that. Money is something I have never needed to think about before but I have woken up from a dream and need to do so now. I will leave you in charge of all the staff, I have complete faith in you as always."

Chalfont gave his little cough and said "I am pleased to do so and thank you My Lady your trust means a great deal."

"I shall have to eat with the guests most of the time I suppose, make appearances so to speak, and yes we need some more staff."

"Mrs Barclay has two nieces that live in the village I believe, she will get them in, she said they were looking for employment only yesterday, that will be a start."

"Excellent, she knows them and what we need."

"Have you finished with your tea My Lady? I will make sure Mr Lakeland's room is ready" said the butler as he cleared the tea things away."

"Oh my yes I had forgotten for a moment, he should be arriving shortly, and yes I think his car is coming up the drive now."

Chapter 3

Archie stepped out of his little sports car and stretched like a cat then he came over and hugged Shelley, being very careful not to crease his coat. They were always delighted to see each other. He looked immaculate as usual, not like Potters who looked like he had been in a fight, he was all hot and bothered . Archie had driven fast all the way and his driving always had this effect on Potters, Archie liked to drive fast and many a chicken and even cyclists and other persona had tales to tell of their encounters.

"Hello old thing how's tricks and why the sudden need of yours truly, no that it's not always good to be back at the old pile?"

Shelley took his arm and walked him into the house after Archie had tossed the car keys to Potters. Chalfont had joined him and gave him a sympathetic look, he had seen Archie drive. Potters got shakily out of the car as though he had faced the fires of hell, he shook himself knowing a glass of something fine awaited him in the butler's pantry in a while. He helped Chalfont with Archie's bags then he drove the car round the back of the hall to where a large airy, dry open sided barn was used to house guest's cars.

"You are in your usual room sir" said Chalfont as he passed Archie.

Archie beamed " What ho, good to feel at home."
Shelley shook his arm "I need your help, advice, well maybe not that as I have already made up my mind what I am going, have to do," she told him confusingly.

Archie looked at her with alarm feeling sure she was up to something he knew that look of old, and he felt sure she was going to drag him into it, like she had so many times before, memories of being in trouble for snitching cakes that were cooling for her to name but a few and of course being far too gallant to ever say it had all been her idea. The were many other things she and Simon had dragged him into. Archie being somewhat of a dandy had always hated getting his clothes dirty or worse torn.

"Don't give me that look" she said scornfully "This is serious I mean life or death."

Archie was now really alarmed and wished he had not agreed to come, but now he thought about it she hadn't given him a chance to refuse, he sighed, he had better listen, although he knew he would be sorry.

Shelley giggled a sound he had not heard from her for a very long time in fact far too long ,in spite of his misgivings he smiled at her, she had won him over as always.

Shelley said "Your face, you look like I am going to ask you to murder someone. How did you guess?"

Archie reeled and stepped back with a gasp. This time Shelley laughed, "Don't worry old thing if I wanted that I would have asked Chalfont, I have a feeling he would do it too, but I think I have already shocked him enough this morning."

Archie's looked at her with horror he was beginning to think the blight Jeremy Coulter had been the one to have a lucky escape after all.

Chalfont announced luncheon was ready. Archie ate nervously so Shelley kindly decided to put him at ease as soon as they were alone. She came straight to the point, "Archie dear I know nothing about cars and you know everything, the thing is I am in desperate need of money and you can sell them for me."

Archie was appalled "In need of money! Sell the collection! How come?"

" Archie please don't, just don't. This is hard enough as it is, but if I don't, I lose Rosewood and I can't I just can't lose any more. My father left very little money it came as a shock and then there were terrible death duties and and the rest."

Archie reached across and patted her hand awkwardly.

"Sorry old thing you had better tell all, and I will see what I can do. Is that err why you agreed to Coulter?

"Yes but I could not go through with it for anything, seeing that face on a daily basis proved to be too much."

He nodded thoughtfully "Makes sense now, wondered why

you agreed to such a blister."

She giggled "Oh Archie I am glad to see you. Well can you help?"

" Yes let me put my mind such as it is to it. Would buy the lot myself if I had the readies, I think we should try and sell as a collection. I work out a value as that and also as individuals. We should be prepared for all. "

"I am keeping one of the Rolls for myself, you can teach me to drive."

"Good idea on both counts."
Chalfont who was just coming to clear started violently and almost dropped his tray he had just been listening to Potter's tale of the drive down and the thought of Lady Shelly driving like that, he made up his mind then and there to teach her himself.

" Would you like coffee served on the terrace My Lady?"

"Yes that would be perfect, the weather is so lovely at present."

"Very good My Lady." Chalfont was pleased to see her smiling again he and all the rest of the staff were glad they would not be losing their places and were determined to make her ideas for their futures work. They had been talking about it and making plans until Mr Potter arrived of course it would not do to discuss the family situation with an outsider until the right moment and that would be after Archie knew.

Shelley and Archie were sitting and enjoying their coffee in the shade on the terrace, looking across the gardens to the lake where they had played as children, they shared the same memories of happy times. Archie sighed in contentment he would help her. He could quite see why she loved the old place, he did himself. Shelley broke the companionable silence.

"There is more Archie, I may as well tell you all, but you can't help me with this bit."

Archie went still, his face locked as if knowing that could not have been all, he should have guessed it had seemed too easy, but she had said whatever it was she didn't need his help, somehow he knew she would.

She told him her plans to making the hall an exclusive guest house, he listened with growing horror yet it made a dreadful sort of sense, a lot of the old families were in the same situation, some were forced to sell homes that had been in their families for generations, he admired her for fighting to hold onto The Hall and taking on all the responsibilities, many girls in her position would have sold the old place given everyone the push and bought a place in London and lived for pleasure alone, finding a rich husband but not her, he should have known she wouldn't, he hadn't realised she had no money to keep it all going. He wasn't really wealthy enough either or he would have helped her out.

"Look here old girl, had no idea things were that bad but you are going to be taking on a whole lot of trouble if you don't get this show spot on don't you know. You can't just let a lot of blighters and bounders in under your roof snitching the silver and whatnots. You can only take on the right sorts of coves."

"Yes I do know that and when we are ready will advertise in the best papers also word of mouth, there are people looking to stay in places like this, genteel country living and they are wealthy enough to pay for the privilege . I only going to take on a small number and they will need to be able to pay in advance fully before they come here."

"The west wing will be off limits and mine alone. The staff will only answer to me, it is going to be hard work but worth it to keep the hall and everyone in it. They have always been so loyal and are quite prepared to do this. I can't just turn my back on them. I won't lose my home I have lost too much already. I have thought and thought and it is the only way believe me, selling the cars will make a big start but I need to keep going. I really haven't a penny to bless myself. I wish there was an easier way but not one I can find. I owe it to us all and all those before me to save Rosewood don't you see? Archie my dearest friend you know without saying your room is always yours and available at all times, Daddy and Simon would have wished that too."

He was very moved and could find no words at first, they would turn in their graves he thought that it should come to this, what happened to all the money? The old Lord had pots of the stuff surely. Yes death duties were dreadfully high that must have been it. Archie knew the old boy was rich at one time he was always living high and well, so was Simon. One did not ask of course but he knew of priceless jewels, where did they go? Her Father had done some kind of favour for a Maharaja Simon had told him, but Archie had at that time fallen madly in love again and hadn't really taken it in, they always seemed up to some dangerous adventure or other, this was just one more and anyway he had just wanted to daydream about the fair Gertrude. He remembered they had been rewarded with a lot of jewels so it must have been something big although he had no idea what. Simon had never told him that bit. Shelley had lived here alone for a year after the accident and had not ventured anywhere so she had not spent it.

"Well old thing if you're set on it and I am not saying I approve because it seems a rummy idea to me I think I can hand you your first guest."

"He is a pal of mine and err also Simon's, a great sort of chap, was a pilot in the war and wounded has a game leg, wounded do you see, and now bit of an invalid and all that, he needs a place like this, fed up of all the females in his family fussing over him and all that rot, bit of a recluse nowadays, just wants peace and quiet, he would be ideal the right sort I mean to say."

"Archie this isn't going to be a nursing home we can't look after the sick and wounded much as I'd like to, there will be no nursing staff to cater for his needs but I thank you all the same."

" No no you read it wrong, my fault, doesn't need special nursing or pap to feed him, has his own man a fellow called Treach, for all that sort of thing if needed, he just needs a quiet place to live for a while, away from aunts and sister fussing about him driving him mad, give him a bit of independence while he gets stronger, he uses a stick to get about he is a good un won't bother you or make off with the spoons. I can bring him down so you can meet him and decide, at least he is one of us, name of James Fitzmichaels the younger son of the Earl of Rogarth."

" I remember Simon speaking of him, very well looks like we have our first guest if he wants to be."

"I will telephone him later and tell him. Now let's go and look at the motors. Tell me when do you want me to start it all taking off? And when do you start your plans?"

"As soon as possible. Chalfont is talking to Mrs Barclay

even as we speak about a couple of new staff and yes keeping the silver safe" she laughed tucking her arm in his as they strolled over to where the cars were housed.

Archie sighed as he gazed at the car collection, "First an auction I think, but first I will talk to some of the chaps in my club. This collection is famous and has been much admired in the past."

"Thank you Archie dear I knew I could rely on you to help me do this painful thing, another link broken you see, but had to be done and I didn't know how. I have no idea about motor cars but as I said earlier I am keeping the Rolls, it has always been my favourite."

Archie approved of this idea. They or rather he inspected the rest. Shelley felt sad but resigned herself to the task she knew it had to done, she did not need the cars and there were those who relied on her, she was glad she had Archie who she would trust with her life if need be, good old and oh so dear friend Archie. She thought herself lucky to have him and such great staff, they were family in a way.

The next day Archie went back to London, this time he let

Potters drive he was tired after spending time with all the cars and talking well into the night with Shelley about holding an auction he needed as he said "To put the old brain to work." He got Potters to drop him off at his club where he found it to be very busy and after he got himself a drink and was welcomed warmly by his pals, he told the tale of the cars to be sold, many were interested in the up coming auction he told them a date had not been set yet for it and he felt sad as he realized the collection would not be able to be kept together, although excited and wanting one of the cars they were much admired it was a fine collection of rare and beautiful motors, none of them could afford all of them, that would take a great deal of money. He had an awkward moment when he saw Jeremy Coulter sitting with a few of his own cronies listening intently, well Archie could not stop any of them bidding in the auction but it would not please him to sell any of his old friend's cars to any of that group.

Archie knew Simon and his father disliked them and would not have let Jeremy marry Shelley but then if they had not died she would not have even considered it, thank God the engagement was over. He was more determined than ever to help her. Still the thought of Coulter driving one of Simon's cars stung. He shuddered at the thought of the pill touching Shelley. But little did he know that had never happened, there had been no show or sign of affection from either party.

    Later Archie invited his good friend James Fitzmichaels round for dinner in his flat he knew James would not want to go anywhere else, he was still recovering and living very quietly at his family's seat. He also wanted to talk to him privately. Archie knew James was in London seeing a specialist about his leg, his man Treach was driving him up to town so after dinner and over a glass of brandy Archie told him about the wonderful opportunity of taking rooms at Rosewood Hall. James was surprised he had known Simon well their love of flying and all motors had made them good friends, he had never met Shelley had only seen a picture but also had never for some reason been to Rosewood, the boys had been to school together of course.

    "I had always thought the family very wealthy, Simon was never short of cash and had anything he wanted, what happened to it all? Seems a bit of an odd show. Rummy!"

" It's a bally mystery old chap and I mean to find out more about it. Can't come right out and ask her but I do know it's missing along with some jewels, uncut stones I think Simon showed me one once. And here's the ideal plan with you down there living in the Hall and keeping an eye on things you might be able to help me find out, that's the beauty of it, you will on the spot to do a little sleuthing, living in your own rooms, I told her you wanted some peace and quiet, would have your own man and not be messed about with and all that rot, so you will be be able to snoop about freely. I can't go and live there she knows I don't need rooms like that and besides I have my own room when I want to visit and I will do often. If I tried to take on more she will think it's charity and she won't have that, no this way is better, what can be wrong with me visiting old chums, what do you say? Simon's sister and all can't let her down."

"Count me in, the truth is I am so bored and stifled can't make a move at home without somebody fussing about, making me rest, they mean well I know but it is trying, enough to drive a chap crazy so this sounds perfect, of course the family won't like it but I can say the quack advised a change of scenery."

"Good show. That's the spirit will do you the world of good I shouldn't wonder, Shelly's a great sport doesn't know what fussing means. You will like her. To finding the treasure," said Archie raising his glass, little did he know he would soon be finding a dead body.

Chapter 4

Shelley sipping her tea that Chalfont had served was looking thoughtful, she missed Archie's company. He was undeniably fun to be with she sighed, she missed her family so much the loving care from her father, her only problems then were whether the new seasons colours would suit her and if her new gown would be ready for some function or other, now none of these things mattered she couldn't remember the last time she had ordered a gown or even went somewhere to wear one. Today she wore an old favourite purple jumper and skirt and as it was cooler and raining sat by a warm fire. She felt lonely.

Chalfont gave a little cough to get her attention

"If I may My Lady I have taken the liberty to draw up a list of requirements we shall need, some new silverware not the finest and some new china it is possibly not prudent to use our priceless family collections for paying guests some of which are family heirlooms and not possible to replace if damaged."

Shelly gave a little start, she had been far away thinking of Simon, Archie and herself as children playing in the gardens.

"Oh Chalfont of course a good idea and one I had not thought of. What would I do without you? She read the list "Yes do get all of this and anything else you think we may need."

" Mrs Barclay has her nieces in and has begun training them as housemaids and she has asked two women to come in from the village to do all the extra laundry if and when we need them. I thought I would go up to town this afternoon and place the orders in Fortnums to be delivered, is there anything you would like me to bring back for you from there My Lady?

" Yes please Chalfont I would like some of those little chocolate truffles, I haven't had any of those in an age. Not since, not since, my father used to always bring me some."

"Very good My Lady, as I am going up so late in the day I think it best if I put up over night in my club, getting the orders right will take some time, it needs to be chosen well to be right for our needs after all."

Chapter 5

Shelley looked surprised Chalfont always seemed to be here at the hall, he did go off with her father from time to time she remembered but otherwise he didn't seem to leave.

"You have a club, but of course you do" she stammered, "Yes of course stay overnight, I know you will get everything right you always do."

"Thank you My Lady." With that Chalfont cleared the tea things away, he had his own plans to fulfil, best not trouble her.

Chalfont took the train to London he soon placed the orders in Fortnum and Masons and some in Harrods and also with the truffles some sugared almonds, he remembered Shelley used to love, he was assured all would be delivered the next day, then he went over into the east end of London, and called into an unsavoury looking pub. He ordered a beer and sat in a dark corner to wait. He didn't have to wait very long. In walked a couple of wiry young men or rather in sauntered , they spotted Chalfont and came over immediately.

"Wotcha Chalfont" they said together.

Chalfont called for a couple more beers. The barmaid brought them over, " Hello beautiful," said one of the brothers.

"Cheek" she answered but she smiled anyway.

When she had walked away swaying her ample hips Chalfont spoke in quiet tones he knew these tough lads well they had worked from time to time for his old master Shelley's Father. These brothers were called Jem and Pete, they didn't know their last name had never met their father and their mother had died when they were boys, they had grown up fast and tough and met Shelley's father when they tried to pick his pockets, he had caught them and he had taken pity on them being so small, thin and obviously hungry so had given the poor filthy little boys some coins and then jobs from time to time. They were very useful and earned their money as they could get into small places when needed and other places after all who would bother to notice yet another scruffy urchin hanging about the streets, they had sharp eyes and ears, when they were chased off they had always done or snitched whatever they were paid to.

They had respected "The Guv" and did all kinds of odd and sometimes shady things for him. They may have been small and wiry, but very strong because Chalfont had seen they were fed, the Guv had paid them well so they they would have done anything for him even murder if asked. They were scruffy but clean and people round here knew not to mess with them. They had earned their respect.

" Sorry about the old Guv he were the best'"

"He didn't go natural did he?"

" No he didn't and the killer hid his tracks well, I haven't been able to find out who because I have been keeping Lady Shelley his daughter safe, doesn't mean I have given up though but she may well possibly be in some danger."

Jem said "Just show me who done it, just give me a crack at them that's all I ask."

"Yeah and me, I'll know what to do about it," snarled Pete menacingly.

Chalfont smiled coldly "Well that leads me nicely into what I was about to ask you to do."

"Anything for you and the old Guv you knows that Mr. Chalfont." they said together.

Chalfont told them about the plan to open the hall as a guest house, they looked puzzled but attentive.

"His Lordship seems to have left her with very little money to keep Rosewood Hall running!"

The brothers looked amazed and said so in their own way. Chalfont put up a hand and took a swift glance there was nobody sitting close enough to hear them.

"Those who killed him haven't got their hands on his store that I am certain of, he liked gold and stones and placed his trust in them, I know he took a payment with them, mark my words they are well hidden somewhere, I have searched without any success to find them for her, my last job for my master is to keep her safe and I intend to do it to the best way I can. Now are you in?"

"What do you want us to do?" asked Pete.

"We are in" said Jem.

"Good Lads I knew I could rely on you, I think the killer will show his hand and we will be ready for him, he thought by killing his Lordship and Simon he would find the treasures, having a free hand so to speak, thinking he would only have a heartbroken girl to deal with, well he is wrong there and made a mistake, but this also proves he knows about His Lordship and his work for the crown and our country and how his Lordship was a little eccentric in his habits also. I think when the Hall is opened up he will try and make his move to search and that my boys will be when we spring and he will pay dearly."

The brothers nodded with grins on their faces that showed somebody was going to get what they had coming to them. Chalfont said "I am in London buying for Rosewood Hall and while here had the happy idea of recruiting my two nephews as new footmen or staff, much needed for the new venture, you will then on the spot to assist and report to me. Keep a close eye on Her Ladyship of course. You will be paid members of staff able to freely be able to move about the hall, any questions just ask me."

"Sounds good to us, a change will do us good," laughed Jem.

"Yea and be just like the old times."

"Let's be off then, grab what you need and meet me at the station, I'll get tickets and supply you with new togs."

The brothers packed a few things in a couple of bags including a few useful tools just in case.

 Soon they boarded the train with Chalfont on their way. All Chalfont's shopping orders would be delivered the next day. They arrived back at the hall where Chalfont introduced his "nephews" to the rest of the staff, and was told the old coach house had be broken into but nothing seemed to be missing and none of the cars were damaged, a tramp looking for shelter was the story being told but Chalfont had different ideas and kept them to himself only talking about his theory and being agreed with by Jem and Pete when they went out to investigate after a cup of strong tea , Jem and Pete had never been to the hall before and were in awe of the whole thing.

Mrs. Barclay who had been told by Chalfont that he was possibly going to bring them back and after that canny man had told her they were motherless lads the old lord had cared about, so she had immediately took them under her ample wing, thinking they were much too thin she had served a huge slice of rich cake to each of them with cups of tea, she vowed to feed them well, they had never been looked after like this before and loved it. Chalfont said "We will just look in the coach house and make sure it's safe Mrs. Barclay before I see her Ladyship."

"I am very glad to see you back Mr Chalfont and no mistake, and those lads of yours, with nasty tramps about and soon strangers here."

Chalfont, Jem and Pete had a good look round they could see the lock was broken, Jem made himself useful by mending it, while Pete had a thorough look round with Chalfont inside and out, watched though they did not know it from an upstairs window by

Shelley, she had been puzzled by the break in and had her own ideas, she was glad Chalfont was back who she trusted completely and she knew her Father had too.

Jem and Pete said "This was a sloppy job too, obviously done and foolish leaving evidence of the break in, nothing took not even tools, he was in a hurry searching, floor all scuffed, we would have left no signs wouldn't have been hard to do after all."

"Yes I agree, it wasn't anyone after the cars, we have to be on our guard my lads. Now to meet her Ladyship, before she dresses for dinner."

Shelley was in the library innocently reading, her two Siamese cats curled up on her lap looking as though they had been there for hours, nobody would have guessed she had been upstairs watching out a few minutes ago.

"Ah Chalfont, I trust all went well in London, you must have heard we have had a mysterious break in."

Jem and Pete stood quietly behind Chalfont they looked at her, she was so like Simon and yet softer and so lovely. They made a silent vow to protect and avenge the daughter of their old saviour

The Guv.

"Yes My Lady I purchased all the things we agreed we would need and took the liberty to bring back my two nephews, I think they will prove most useful and are in fact in need of work. May I introduce Jem and Pete. They worked for your father sometimes when he needed them too" said Chalfont smoothly.

Shelley looked at the two handsome young men, they did once have footmen but they had gone off to war and had not like so many returned.

"Well done good thinking, I believe we will be in need of them, and Chalfont you have never mentioned you had nephews before. Welcome to Rosewood Hall Jem and Pete, I hope you will be happy here." She smiled at them.

That was it, they saw her Father's wicked smile and were lost in it, two tough young men who would do her bidding just as they had done his willingly.

"Thank you My Lady" they both said shyly. Chalfont led them out and gave them rooms in the servants quarters near his, he also gave them some uniforms, dark trousers and very dark brown jackets, colours that easily blended into the shadows, also soft soled shoes for indoors to move silently about, they smiled and nodded, just like old times and they had missed them. This would suit them very well indeed. They looked very smart and made the young maidservants hearts flutter.

Chapter 6

Shelley telephoned Archie and told him about the break in, he cursed silently under his breath,so the bounder had started, "I say old girl are you feeling well, not frightened or any of that rot, Chalfont there?"

"Of course silly, although Chalfont was in London when we think it happened, he's back now and has brought his two nephews with him as new footmen or something like, a good idea and one I had not thought of" she said lightly. "We think it was probably a tramp looking for somewhere to sleep, nothing was stolen or damaged, and one of Chalfont's nephews has mended the lock. Useful sort of chap."

Archie was thinking fast he was sure Chalfont had never mentioned nephews but then why would he, it seemed rummy to him and so was this break in, he didn't like the sound of any of it. He did not want to alarm Shelley though, a woman and all alone, he had forgotten she was in a house with loyal staff all around her and also didn't know because she had carefully not told him she had also got her father's gun with her, loaded and in her bedroom, Simon had taught her how to use it as well as how to fight, use a sword and knife as a good brother should in her opinion. She had never needed to but she began to understand why he had done so. There was a mystery surrounding his and her father's deaths and she meant to find out what, also the break in was fishy. She did not believe the tramp story that was Barky's theory.

Archie told her he would be down shortly bringing his friend James, who he was waiting for. They would motor down together and arrive late, James he told her was all for the whole idea and he Archie ,was sure she would like his friend. Archie would feel better when James and his man Treach were down there. James was a good sort and brave too.

"He's a quiet sort of cove, won't know he's there, Treach his man takes care of him" he assured her. Soon they were driving down to meet her in Archie's car with Potters and Treach following in James's car with luggage.

They arrived late but Shelley was waiting up for them in her little sitting room, she presented a cosy pretty picture curled up in an armchair reading before a warm fire eating some of the rich chocolate truffles Chalfont had brought back from London for her. James thought she was very lovely and watched her shyly. Archie walked towards the fire hands outstretched "It's a bit parky out there tonight that fire is most welcome I approve wholeheartedly."

"Then you will approve of this too." She rang for Chalfont but he was already coming through the door and laden with another tray was Jem, he placed it carefully on a table, hot tea and a plate sandwiches were a welcome sight.

"I have placed Mr Fitzmichael in a room next to you for tonight sir, your bags have been taken up, fires have been lit as it has turned a little chilly. Your man has taken the little dog up now."

"Chalfont I say it again you are one of the real wonders of the world."

"Thank you sir." He and Jem left.

Archie introduced James to Shelley properly at last as they tucked into their supper. James took her warm little hand in his and smiled shyly at her he felt strangely tongue tied in front of this beautiful vivacious girl. Shelley instantly liked this tall thin fair haired young man, her first guest had arrived. What really sealed it was her two Siamese cats took an instant liking to him and settled comfortably on his lap.

The next morning James was given his own suite of rooms to settle into, they overlooked the small lake in the distance much to his liking, he had brought his spaniel Toby with him and he was well content. Archie was staying on for a few days too. They all met up for breakfast to make plans, Treach would move and unpack James's belongings. Chalfont had waited to see if he was really staying before installing him in one the suite of rooms they had chosen for the new guests. James thanked Shelley for letting him stay, she told him she was pleased to have him and hoped to hear tales of him and Simon.

Toby adored Shelley and after some rude swearing and growling from Sassy and Tazraz, the Siamese cats chose to ignore him walking away in disgust when he tried to make friends with them.

Shelley, Archie and James went for a walk in the crisp Autumn morning air, Toby bounding along with them, Shelley was pointing out the boathouse and telling James he could take the boat out whenever he wanted also they had a stretch of river he could use that belonged to the hall, he was watching her closely as she talked to him, he thought she looked perfect, be careful he told himself he would enjoy his stay here.

Shelley was wearing a russet coloured coat and a small close fitting hat over her golden curls, she looked beautiful these colours suited her, she felt happier than she had done for a long time, alive and no longer alone, it was a misty cool morning and she was enjoying their company. She had plans for the future again. Archie spoke to James who was busy listening to Shelley and didn't hear him.

Archie spoke again "James your dog is kicking up the most frightful racket, seems to be coming from the boathouse." The two men set off to find out what Toby was barking at, probably a rabbit thought Shelley following them unconcerned also although Archie had dashed off James with his injured leg could only follow slowly she followed James she liked this shy young man and did not want to make him feel uncomfortable in front of her. When she reached the boathouse Toby had stopped barking and was whining next to James who was looking grave, Archie was looking shocked and very pale as he held up a hand, "Shelley don't go in there stay back" he said in an unlike Archie voice, she had never heard him speak like this before.

"What is wrong? What has happened? Archie tell me at once" she demanded trying to step forward, a gentle but firm arm held her back and she looked into James's dark blue eyes. He shook his head and told her softly " A dead body, not a sight for a lady."

Shelley was torn between pushing past to see for herself

and staying in the oddly comforting place of his arm that he had round her still. Archie knowing her well said "You really don't want to venture in there old thing believe me." Both men had seen bodies before from the war but this one right on their doorstep shocked them both. It was a nasty sight. A brutal end.

"We must call the rozzers at once" said Archie.

James agreed, reluctantly taking his arm from Shelley.

"Why? She asked , whether to ask about the body or James's removal of that comforting arm she could not have answered.

James was quiet, letting Archie answer, he felt unsettled having held her even for that moment and thought the news would come better from Archie her old friend anyway.

"He whoever he was, err, was murdered, my dear old thing we have to call them." Archie took her arm and started back towards the house.

"Are you sure?" she asked is a subdued voice.

"Very sure old thing."

James followed them with his now very quiet little dog.

"Was it the tramp do you think Archie? I mean it wasn't someone we knew was it?

"Would be hard to tell" answered Archie without thinking, he saw Shelley's face as she clutched his arm. "I mean to say, didn't see the tramp's face of course but yes I think so, it wasn't somebody we know judging by his togs."

They had reached the house and Archie went to phone the police calling for a stiff snifter after.
Shelley led James to the library and rang to Chalfont. "Please bring some coffee , did Archie tell you what happened?"

"Yes My Lady" he answered pouring out three brandies. "I will bring in the coffee shortly." He handed them a glass each. They had sat down, "Oh James I am so sorry, this was such a horrid start to your quiet life here. It isn't usual for dead bodies to appear in front of my family."

Chalfont who was passing through the doorway raised his eyebrows but she did not see that.

Chapter 7

"Oh no!" wailed Shelley suddenly. Archie coming back and picking up his his brandy asked "What is it?"

"Americans" she cried.

"What about them?" he asked in a puzzled voice wondering if the shock had got to her.

"I forgot to tell you with all that has happened, Aunt Georgia is sending a very rich American and his wife down tomorrow, they are on a tour of sorts and want to stay here for three months, they are excited about living in an old place like the hall, she says they are they very thing, nice people and are paying well, they arrive tomorrow, she showed them pictures and that was all it took. Oh bother why did a tramp decide to get murdered in my boathouse? They won't stay now."

James gave her a little smile "I don't think he had much choice in the matter."

They were just finishing lunch when the police turned up.

"Shall I serve coffee in the library My Lady?" Chalfont was his usual cool self although all the other servants had been gossiping about the murder. He himself had without a word been down to take a look at the corpse saw at once the murderer hadn't wanted his victim to be identified. Nothing in any pockets either.

"Yes please Chalfont and bring in two extra cups."

"Yes My Lady, Inspector Riley and Sargent Mathers." The two policemen followed the three into the library took offered seats and thanked Shelley for the offer of coffee. Inspector Riley was a tall thin man with reddish hair and moustache, Sargent Mathers was a big jolly looking man.

"I understand you discovered the body, said Inspector Riley

to Archie.

"It was actually my dog Toby" answered James. Toby had been given a snack from the kitchen and was sleeping up in James new sitting room.

"I was the first person to find the awful thing, the dog was creating a dreadful racket and who could blame him!" said Archie.

"Quite, can you tell me what you did then?"

"Looked in through the door spotted the poor blighter, stepped back out smartish to prevent Shelley seeing it."

The Sargent was busy writing in his notebook.

"You didn't go in any closer, touch anything or think to make sure the victim was beyond help."

"Believe me I saw that he was beyond all help, the war and all that, and so my thoughts were best to get Shelley away back to the house and phone you."

"I see very commendable I am sure. Did anything about the body seem familiar?" said Riley glancing at Shelley.

"Never saw the fellow before in my life" answered Archie quickly

"You Sir? Riley asked James.

"I didn't see him, too busy giving my arm to Shelley, also my dog was distressed, saw the best thing to do was what Archie suggested, couldn't help the poor fellow after all so came back here."

"So nobody entered or disturbed the crime scene, good. Will you take us and show us where this all took place."

"One moment Inspector Riley," put in Shelley quickly she had been silent, sipping her coffee and listening until now, both the policemen looked at her, "There is one more thing to add and may be relevant, yesterday morning while Archie was away meeting James to bring him down here, the gardener discovered that the old coach house that houses my late Father's collection of rare motor cars had been broken into. Nothing had been stolen or damaged luckily."

"Well now My Lady" said Sergeant Mathers. "You didn't think to report this?"

"No not really we just thought it might be a passing tramp looking for somewhere to sleep, it happens sometimes but they usually sleep in an old shed far away from the house and are no bother to anybody, didn't want to waste your time. The servants tried to reassure me but somehow I didn't quite believe that a tramp would bother to break a lock when there are several barns and outhouses that could be used more easily and have straw and what not."

Four men stared at her warily with new respect. Chalfont who was clearing the coffee things and going out of the door sniggered silently to himself she was her Father's daughter right enough.

"As I said nothing stolen or damaged except the lock, so no need to trouble you then, but this might be connected."

Riley said "We will take a look at the coach house after viewing the body."

The four men rose and Shelley did too, "I am coming with you, I have no desire to see the body but all the rest yes." They didn't argue with her knowing she wouldn't take any notice if they did.

Coats were donned and out they all went. They went down

to the boat house first, followed by two Siamese cats who decided that as the dog was missing they would do their own investigating with Shelley who they adored. When they got there Shelley stayed back playing with her cats by waggling a leafy twig at them, she was listening hard to what the men said though.

Archie and James were asked to wait outside not to disturb any clues, the two policemen stepped inside leaving the doors open. As soon as they got close to the corpse they looked and nodded to each other, they thought they knew who it was.

They would need to make sure.
They made a search of the boathouse while the others waited outside impatiently. Sargent Matthers spotted a crowbar tossed in a dark corner Chalfont had already seen it and left it for them to find, he did not think it was the murder weapon not enough blood on it, he thought it was used to damage the victim's face though.

"Looks like you found the murder weapon you old bloodhound. Nothing else of any use to us here, call the lads in to remove the body."

Shelley shivered even though she was wearing her russet

woollen coat this was beastly, a human being had been killed in her boathouse somewhere she and Simon had played as children it felt contaminated somehow now. She was angry. The policemen came out of boathouse joined Archie and James who was now leaning heavily on his stick, he was feeling suddenly very tired, Shelley glanced at him and was careful not to show concern. They walked towards her, Riley saying "The victim was murdered without any doubt , and I think My Lady, was possibly connected to the break in of your coach house, we will look at that now."

"So you recognized the murder victim," remarked James.

"I wouldn't like to say yet for sure but possibly, it is of course not a sure thing this early in the investigations" replied Riley.

The three friends nodded. They all walked to the coach house letting Shelley lead the way, after all it was her home.

"Was he a dangerous criminal, the murder victim you may have recognized?" she asked innocently, or so she thought. Riley was not fooled, "No we think it maybe a petty thief not usually this far from town" he answered equally innocently. The others pricked up their ears at this news. Chalfont was there with Pete unlocking the doors, "I took the liberty My Lady feeling sure the police officers would wish to investigate here too."

"As usual you are right Chalfont."

Matther's took a long look at Pete who knew he was too, but did not stop or look back him, Pete acted as he belonged here a valued member of staff wearing his house uniform without a care in the world, he unlocked the door and stepped confidently inside with Chalfont. He was forgotten immediately as Riley and Matthers saw the car collection.

"Oh my what beauties!" they both said.
Riley said "You are sure nothing has been stolen. "Not even something small and seemingly unimportant?"

Shelley replied "Not as far as I am aware of."

"Seems a bit odd, but maybe he and his chum had a falling out before they could"
Matthers replied "Perhaps he was checking the lay of the land and intended to come back later."

"Doesn't explain why he was murdered though. Well we

had better get it searched and printed, and after photographed the body will be removed later today, Lady Sheringham."

"Thank goodness for that, this is all rather horrid, it doesn't make sense and I am sorry it happened at my home."

"We will try to be finished as quickly as possible My Lady, may I suggest you go back to the house in the warm, we won't disturb you."

Chapter 8

"Oh Lord I have more of my guests arriving soon, bother they will probably turn and run for the hills, how annoying to have a murder to explain, I had better go and see to it myself, what a beastly thing to have happened." With that Shelley began to go back to the house to prepare herself for the upcoming ordeal telling Chalfont to get tea and coffee arranged, she said quietly "Archie, James, can you have another look at the cars and see if we missed anything, when the Inspector has finished of course?"

They were only too pleased not wanting to be part of her guest interview that was to be a bit tricky and best handled by her.

Inspector Riley smiled to himself understanding them perfectly.

Then the sound of his team and the ambulance turning up caught his attention.

"Please don't touch anything else until it has been checked for possible outsider prints but it's a bit late for that now after all these footprints everywhere," he said.

James had moved over to three packing cases that were securely fastened down and had gratefully sat down on one, his leg was aching.

Inspector Riley had told Sargent Matthers to show the team where the body was. He and Archie were looking around the floor when he exclaimed after moving some old sacking "Well look what we have here, some blood stains not a great deal but looks like our corpse may have come to grief in here, possibly a fight started, enough blood for him to have died in here."

"The doctor when he has finished over yonder will be able to tell us more. I shall stroll over and see him at the boathouse." Archie said meaningfully "We will lock up when you have finished, these cars are worth a small fortune and they don't have a mark on any of them."

"I understand perfectly sir, our team will clean up."
Just then "Jem strolled in saying "Her Ladyship charged me with making sure there was no scratch left on these here motors of hers, and I was to lock up too."

Riley nodded with a laugh. "Of course."
Chalfont's work thought Archie good man, he was feeling cold himself

"Come on James old man, we are redundant let's go back to your rooms and get some tea."
So that's what they did, Archie would have liked to hear what the police doctor said but he could see James was tired and he also suspected that the doctor would only speak to the Inspector when they were out of earshot.

Shelley after tidying herself up had met and was now having tea served to a large friendly American and his equally large and pleasant wife. Hiram B Snyder was an American millionaire who owned a film studio in Hollywood, and his wife

Charlene had been a film star when he met and swept her off her feet. He had a mop of white hair and twinkling blue eyes, and his wife was still very beautiful with a little help from a good famous beauty house. She was beautifully dressed and well made up with carefully styled golden blonde hair. They were both delighted to be at Rosewood Hall they told Shelly as they shook her hand.

"Well this is a mighty fine old house and my wife and I are looking forward to staying here as long as we are in in England," said Hiram beaming at Shelley.

"It is so beautiful" agreed Charlene in her soft voice and Southern accent.

"Everything is so darn green, I've never seen so many shades of green" said Hiram.

Shelley sighed softly as she watched Chalfont serve them cups of tea and dainty cucumber sandwiches.

"I am delighted to see you here," Shelly said softly "I have to tell you though that the police are outside here searching the grounds. Oh dear I so sorry, this sort of thing just doesn't happen, but you see a body has been found in the boathouse."

"Oh my" said Charlene.

"Lady Sherringham, well that's just wonderful ! A British murder, a real who done it murder!" exclaimed Hiram excitedly, "Well this I got to see."

Shelley stared at him in amazement she had expected them to turn around and leave immediately. Perhaps this would turn out well after all.

"Who is the stiff anyone you know" asked Hiram.

"Stiff?" asked Shelly.

"Corpse" answered Hiram.

"Oh I see, no nobody anyone here knew."

"Hiram wants to make a film of a British murder mystery you see Lady Shelly" explained Charlene quickly.

"Yeah and you handed me one right in my hand, what a piece of luck and as it wasn't a family member, and you didn't know the guy, was it a guy by the way? I can see first hand how things work over here, get some ideas. This is some sweet break." Shelley still looked astonished but Charlene laughed "I guess it is Honey."

"You still want to stay?"

"You bet and even more now."

"I will take you out to meet them."

Chalfont suddenly appeared with Shelly's coat, he always knows what is going on Shelley thought, then Charlene slipped her furs back over her shoulders and Hiram was eager to be off.

"Say how well do you know the butler guy?"

"I have known him all my life" Shelley answered somewhat startled.

It was getting chilly outside and Archie who was watching from James's room's window said "What the devil is she up to now?" and dashed down to join them.

"Hello there," he called as he strolled to meet them.

"Archie this is Hiram and Charlene my new guests, and Hiram makes films, he is interested in making a murder mystery" said Shelley making a strange screwed up face behind the American's back at Archie, who understood immediately knowing her so well. She was confused and surprised that the American's were still happy to stay.

"Howdy" said the big friendly American.

"Hi" said his lovely wife.

"They want to see where it happened."

"Nothing easier you came to the right place" said Archie cheerfully. "This is where the body was discovered but our boys in blue or rozzers are still searching for clues so we will have to be careful don't you know."

"Rozzers?" asked Hiram.

"Police" answered Archie happily.

He had pointed to two constables looking around outside the boathouse. "I will show you inside tomorrow when they have pushed off."

"Sure thing" said Hiram watching the police eagerly.

Shelly and Charlene passed a look that said very clearly, men.

"Any idea who he was?"

Archie said "Possibly a petty thief."

Hiram looked somewhat disappointed.

"After the famous car collection" said Archie hastily seeing his face.

"My late father has car collection it's in the old coach house , we think he was on the lookout, the coach house has been broken into, it is all a mystery. We will show you inside tomorrow. We can go over there just to see if you like."

"That's more like it" breathed Hiram. He went over and spoke to the constable. "Say found any clues?" he asked them in his friendly way.

They straightened up "Not really sir as somebody has been tramping about all over," one of them said reproachfully looking over at Archie.

"And with a dog looks like" said the other

"I say we weren't to know people were going to leave corpses around, we found the thing too, or rather the dog did". Shelley said quickly "Constables when you have finished cook will give you tea." She also thought Chalfont will want to know what they have if anything found.

"Very good My Lady very kind I'm sure" said the constables who had heard about Mrs. Barclay's famous cakes from his sister in the village.

When Shelley led them to the coach house however it was still occupied by Inspector Riley and Sergeant Mathers who were busy talking to two more constables, Jem was arms folded leaning against the door watching their every move with a dark look of suspicion on his face and thoroughly enjoying every moment. The inspector said "We are nearly finished here for tonight, your man can lock up for now, I'll be back in the morning and will need to interview everyone, all members of staff too of course.

"Of course Inspector Riley, my footman here will see to it" answered Shelley. "Good night see you in the morning."

"Good night My Lady." The police nodded at the others, Jem locked up muttering under his breath after making sure the police saw him checking the cars before they left. He really was enjoying himself. He began whistling cheerfully.

"We will show you the cars tomorrow the light will be better then too" said Shelley.

As it was getting dark the party made their way back to the house, a chilly damp mist was in the air.

Chapter 9

Charlene pulled her furs around herself closer and shivered she wasn't used to this cold damp Autumn weather as she lived in California but on the other hand she didn't get too many chances to wear this coat, she was also enjoying herself enormously and loved the idea of living in this beautiful old English house and also her Hiram was really excited and happy. She was recovering from a serious illness and needed to rest and recover, another reason they had come to stay here in the countryside. She only hoped the house was warmer than out here. She needn't have worried, when she and Hiram went up to their rooms a maidservant was putting coals onto the already brightly burning fire in the fireplace. The rooms looked warm and cosy and welcoming. Hiram looked round again with pleasure.

"Well Honey I reckon we struck gold here, I wanted to make a classy British mystery murder and we stepped right slap dang into the real thing, of course we'll have to get it written a sight more interesting story but that's no problem, the main thing is I can get to watch the British police at work first hand and that will be really something to see I can tell you. I have a mind to send for Miss Renner my secretary to take notes, and Dirk Montana to come here and soak up the atmosphere as I have him in mind to play the hero. What do you say? Looks there is plenty of rooms."

"That is a swell idea baby but you need to check it out with Lady Shelly first. She is so sweet and kind."

"Yeah you got that right baby, this place is so big and everything so old but she is such smart girl, looks like she is fighting to hold onto the place and who can blame her. These rooms are really swell"

"Poor little thing her Pa died and all, her aunt told me when she talked about us getting a chance to stay here, and she is so sweet to us and all, it was the taxes, it might help her get by if we can bring them down, we'll ask her later."

"Taxes !" snorted Hiram, always a sore point. " Yeah but these aristocrats have to be treated just so, she will be proud so I'll ask her as a huge favour to me, and it will be" he said wisely.

"Honey she will love Dirk everyone loves movie stars and he will set himself up to charm."

"He will have to be warned to lay off the booze" said Hiram darkly.

"Honey we need to dress for dinner, I shall ring for Miriam, I have a notion to wear my diamonds tonight."

Shelley with the help of Polly dressed carefully she was very thoughtful, she was thinking about James, she found him interesting, she had made up her mind to ask Archie more about him, she remembered Archie telling her that James had injured his leg in the war a flying accident, and wanting to get away from his fussing female relatives so she made up her mind not to ask him or fuss, but she had only been half listening to Archie at the time he had recommended James as one of his friends and that had been good enough for her then but now she was curious about him. Polly brought the dark yellow silk evening gown over from the wardrobe and helped her into it, the gown was severely cut very plain but fitted her so well showing off her lovely figure. Shelley had not really bothered to dress up for dinner or anything else for quite a while and she looked back at herself in the mirror, she saw a pale young woman with very dark blue rather sad eyes, red gold wavy hair, she smiled at herself and said "Hello welcome back time to start living again."

"You look beautiful My Lady, good to see you smiling again, it is really." .

"Thanks Polly, you needn't wait up for me I can easily manage and with all the guests you will be needed elsewhere, you can go on now."

Polly bobbed a little curtsy and left very pleased to be able to report downstairs that Her Ladyship was looking a rare treat and no mistake. She would hold her own with them film people although it was exciting them being here, little did she know what was coming.

Shelley brushed her hair and put a small diamond and amber clip in her curls, she fastened a dainty matching necklace around her neck and bracelet around her wrist it was made to look like tiny daisies. With diamond petals and an amber centre, it had been a birthday present from her father. She dusted a little powder over her face, she wore a dark peach lipstick and she was done. She picked up a velvet wrap that matched her gown and made her way downstairs.

Archie and James were waiting for her, Archie grinned delighted to have his old friend back as herself again, James thought she looked beautiful but she would never be interested in an old crock like himself. a man with a game leg who needed a stick to get about he decided to keep his feelings to himself he was in enough pain as it was.

James was wrong she thought the brave Englishman who had been wounded defending their country looked very handsome in his dark evening clothes setting off his ash blonde hair, one lock falling forward across his forehead, she had a sudden urge to touch it. Archie looked immaculate as always his dark locks gleaming under the light. She linked arms with both of them smiling and they went into the library for drinks and to wait for the others.

Hiram and Charlene soon joined them, the big American beaming with delight and Charlene looking elegant in her gown of ruby velvet and her magnificent diamonds shone like stars. They were all looking forward to a cosy evening getting to know each other better.

Mrs. Barclay had surpassed herself presenting them with a wonderful dinner and she in honour of the American guests cooked what she called a good old real English dinner, a traditional classic roast beef with all the trimmings, after that a warming plum pie with cream for dessert. Drinks and laughter flowed. James watched Shelley from the corner of his eye when he thought she wasn't watching, her eyes sparkled when she laughed, she is not for me he thought sadly. Some lucky blighter will win her heart.

The ladies moved to the drawing room and made themselves comfortable in front of the huge log fire. The men were left to their cigars and brandy.

"Say do you think we can get into the coach house tomorrow? I sure would like to see inside that place if the cops are done with it. The Inspector says he'll be glad to talk to me and answer some things about British police methods."

"Shouldn't be a problem and he seems to be a decent sort of cove" answered Archie.

"You'll get to see the magnificent motors too" said James quietly.

" You sure are saying a lot about them I look forward to seeing them . About that do you guys think that is behind the murder?"

"Sure to be I should say" said Archie.

"Then I am looking forward to seeing those cars and that's for sure."

They after each giving some more ideas about the possible cause of the murder joined the ladies for coffee.

Later that night when she though everyone else was fast asleep Shelly dressed herself in some of Simon's black black trousers and a black sweater. She took a black knitted hat and tucked her red gold hair tightly under it.

She crept downstairs softly listening for any sounds but all was quiet. Her two Siamese cats slunk along beside her delighted to have their beloved all to themselves and even more to be going on a nocturnal adventure. Hunting for something that hopefully squeaked, they were silent. The three of them reached the front hall, where Shelley had picked up the lantern that was kept by the front door. Tazrazz growled softly and then so did Sassy, Shelly stiffened she had heard something too, it was the sound of a door closing quietly upstairs, of course somebody might be using the lavatory but she darted followed by the cats into the library, feeling slightly foolish after all why shouldn't she move around her own house in the middle of the night with her cats but dressed like this would look very strange. She opened the door a crack and listened all was quiet so with lantern lit now in hand she unlocked the French windows onto the terrace and silently crept out, her cats after bunting her legs lovingly darted out sniffing and exploring delighted with this wonderful new game.

Chapter 10

Shelly had armed herself with keys headed for the coach house. She didn't know she had been seen by Jem who is taking turns with Pete keeping watch at night. Jem slipped silently back to where Chalfont and Pete were having a late drink before going to bed.

"Lady Shelly is having a little look around the coach house with them couple of viscous cats of hers for company, I thought you should know. I can't see an signs of anyone else"

Chalfont chortled "She is like her father and brother to be sure, we had better keep a close eye on her though, never know who else might be about hidden around best be absolutely sure. You did right to tell me." Chalfont picked up a truncheon, the others had a cosh each and the three of them slipped out of a back door and keeping well into the shadows they made their way around and stood in some shrubs under a tree to keep watch.

Soon they saw Archie creeping along the side of the house making for the coach house too.

"What the?" began Pete but then he saw Clalfont silently chortling, "Don't worry" he whispered " He is harmless."

Archie was in fact armed with the poker from his bedroom, he was also feeling puzzled for the coach house key was missing from it's usual hook and so he was creeping along with the poker ready to do battle if needed. "Aha!" he said to himself as he could see a faint moving light coming from one small window of the coach house. "Some blighter is messing about in there and I'll catch them red handed."

He stole silently up to the door which was open slightly and he tried to creep in only to be greeted with a welcoming yowl from Tazrazz. Archie dropped the poker in surprise with a clatter and

Tazrazz spat and swore with annoyance this was not the response to his friendly greeting he had expected, he thought his old friend Archie had come to join in the fun not throw noisy objects at him. Shelley shrieked and dropped the lantern which luckily didn't smash but did go out.

"I say old thing what the dickens are you doing out here, might have given me a heart attack don't you know."

"Archie what are you doing following me?" she asked suspiciously.

"I wasn't following you or rather didn't know it was you I was following, I heard noises and the rest you know, thought some blighter was here having another pop at the motors."

Shelly who was standing with her hand on her heart trying to stop it pounding suddenly giggled. "Oh Archie how brave you are, well it was only me and I'm jolly cold so let's go back in there's nothing to see out here and besides the lamp's gone out."

"I am all for that, it's turned really chilly tonight."

Archie took the key and they went back after he locked up. At the sound of Shelly's shriek Jem and Pete had rushed over to come to her aid but Chalfont who knew of Archie and Shelly's escapades of old slowly followed them shaking his head, then the three of them hid listening and laughing quietly watching Archie and Shelly go back to the house followed by the disappointed cats who would have liked to play a little longer. Archie and Shelly went into the drawing room both feeling cold and knowing the fire would still be warm.

"Look here my dear old girl meandering about in the dark of the night is not a good idea, there is a dangerous murderer at large please promise you won't do it again, I admit you'd be a beautiful corpse but not one I'd jolly well want to find. Rather fond of you don't you know."

Shelly was torn between annoyance at having her investigation curtailed and a warm feeling that Archie was brave and caring enough to venture out to see what was going on. "I won't be afraid of walking freely and protecting my own home, I refuse to let that happen."

Before a lively debate started there came a discreet knock on the door, it was then opened by Chalfont bearing a tray on which rested two cups of hot chocolate. Two pairs of eyes looked at him, he gave his little cough and said "I heard you go out and come back in My Lady and thought you might be needing this to warm you." He also had two dishes of chopped meat that he put down for the cats who greeted him with a yowl of pleasure.

Shelley had thrown off her hat at Archie laughed and said "Thank you Chalfont very well I give in and won't go wandering with all of you keeping guard I won't need to but I want to be aware of what is up and included."

"Very good My Lady and if I may add very wise until the murderer is caught." He didn't mention or need to that Jem and Pete were watching and guarding.

Shelly stretched and yawned then after she had finished her hot chocolate followed by the cats went back to her bed, she gave Archie a sisterly hug and a peck on the cheek, they had done this since childhood. They were truly very fond of each other.

"Good night old thing" he whispered as they went up the stairs to their own rooms.

Chapter 11

The next morning was one of those beautiful golden Autumn days almost as if summer was reluctant to leave, Polly after bringing in Shelly's morning tea drew the curtains letting in the sunlight, both cats jumped off the bed and streaked through the door to go downstairs, Shelley opened one eye.

"Good morning My Lady it's a beautiful one."
Shelley tried to bury her head in her pillows and snuffled "Nonsense it can't be morning yet I only just closed my eyes."

Polly laughed and laid out some clothes. Shelley wore a dark yellow cashmere sweater over a brown silk shirt and a brown skirt and stockings, she added some of her amber earrings that showed off her pretty hair so well, a light dusting of powder and a little lipstick and she was ready for breakfast.

Archie, James and Hiram were already tucking in. they stood as she entered but she waved them back down to enjoy their meal. Chalfont served her with fresh tea and toast. Hiram informed them that Charlene was breakfasting in bed as she always did and would join them later, but he was ready and raring to go.

Shelly laughed "After we have finished dress up warmly the sun might be shining but it won't be very warm, we will take you over to the coach house, the police have finished there but will be back later this morning I understand."

"You are in for a rare treat when you see the motors" said James with his shy smile. "They are real beauties."

"Yes enjoy and admire them while you can, next week they go under the hammer" added Archie.

"Say what do you mean by that?" asked Hiram.

"I am putting them up for sale, well all except my Rolls Royce Phantom it has always been my favourite and I cannot bear to part with it, besides I must have a car. The others just sit there looking beautiful."

"They need to be with someone who really appreciates them," said James.

Hiram didn't say a word just nodded his head.

Hiram looked puzzled but decided to ask Archie about it later. The men were wearing coats already but Shelley went to get one of hers.

"Say what's all this about Lady Shelley selling her Daddy's cars. Is she really in that much of financial trouble?

"Yes sadly like so many others, she was hit by huge death duties when her father and brother were killed, she is selling the cars to keep the house going, Rosewood Hall has been in her family for generations, she will fight like the dickens to keep it that way."

"That's a real shame, we guessed it was that way for her, to take us."

"She's coming" hissed James who turned to greet her with a smile, she looked all golden and Autumn herself, dressed in the colours of the turning leaves he thought. They all made their way to the coach house. Shelley unlocked the doors and they all stepped inside.

The big American was speechless, he shook his head as if to clear it and make sure he was really seeing what he thought he was seeing, then he whistled.

"Lady Shelley" he croaked "No auction, there will be no auction, no sir, these babies are mine every last one of these beauts, you got my word on it just name the price that 's all I am asking, name the price I won't argue none, I just got to have them."

Shelley blinked in amazement and then said "Archie had them valued he will tell you. You really mean to keep the collection whole, oh I am so delighted to hear that, it means so much to me."

He held out a huge hand and she put her tiny one in it they shook on it.

"Just let anyone try and stop me keeping them together that's what I am saying." He walked around gazing in reverence and adoration at his new collection.

"Hoowee baby mine all mine! I'll ship them home and love them like they was my children."

Shelley had to keep her tears in check, this had to be done and at least her father's cars were staying together and going to a good home where they would be loved like he had done, cared for, and also no horrid auction something she had dreaded , watching her father's precious cars being haggled over like part of his memory and sold one by one, no not now, smile and no tears she thought, but her eyes were bright and James noticed, he wanted to hug her but did not dare.

Chalfont gave a little cough behind them and said "My Lady, Shall I serve coffee in the morning room."

"Thank you Chalfont" she said pulling herself together, "I will be right there."

Archie was telling Hiram the cost of the cars he nodded happily without a quibble and said he would see to it at once, "Now you go cancel that auction son."

Archie laughed and they went into the house together talking Archie vowed to telephone and cancel the auction right away.

Shelley slipped her hand through James's arm and they wandered back to the house together, she thought how he had held her in his arms and it had been so nice but now he was so aloof, very proper of course. She intended to find out why because she thought he had seemed to have been interested in her, but now was probably now a good time and he had dark shadows under his eyes poor love, did he have somebody? She would ask Archie he was sure to know. They went to talk to the police again and have coffee too. James felt absurdly happy to have her all to himself even for a little while. Archie had told him how he had found her last night in the coach house making sure the cars were safe.

"Little fathead out there when a murderer might still be about," grumbled Archie.

James replied "What an amazing woman, you can't blame her for defending her home, shows real spirit."

"Not if it gets her murdered, we shall have to keep a close eye on her and other things, she always was full of mischief even as a toddler up to all kinds of larks just as bad as Simon. I always thought the nursemaid had to be nippy. Shelley's husband when she finds one will surely had his hands full. He will need to be a brave soul I can tell you"

James thought about that with a pang he would be a lucky man to win her heart whoever it may turn out to be.

"Have you never thought about it yourself, I mean to say being so close as you are and all that" he finished a bit flustered.

Archie laughed "No fear! Good lord no, I love her dearly Simon's sister and all that, nothing I wouldn't do for her of course, that goes without saying, she is the best of girls, like a sister to me, I will protect her but she is stubborn and feisty would run rings round me never thought of her as a wife for me. I would want a peaceful home."

James could not explain to himself how relieved he was to hear these words. He had watched the real affection between Shelley and Archie and had wondered if it might mean more.

"Well I must say I wish I had part of your little party last night, sounds like fun was had by one and all."

"No such thing, it was cold and damp and not a thief in

sight thank goodness, but I will tell you one thing rather strange Chalfont was on to us, was waiting with hot cocoa when we got in, said he had heard her go out, I wouldn't put it past him to have followed her either, or else sent one of those new chaps he has brought in, he seems pretty pally with them too when I come to think about it. I think it is better that you are fresh and alert this morning."

"Why do you think Chalfont might be up to no good?" asked James in surprise.

"Oh no not him. he is loyal through and through but he is up to or suspects something, knows more than he is letting on."

James nodded thoughtfully "Yes it looks like you are right, I wonder what though, there is definitely more going on here than we know about, we shall just have to find out what."

Chapter 12

Archie was right about Chalfont, Jem and Pete had taken a good look at the body and had recognized him as a thief they knew from the past in London.

"Not a bad sort he was, no violence or rough stuff, he was shy of gangs or anything like that, he has worked for a couple of nobs in the past though, thieving for them and getting paid for his trouble,"

"None too bright though he stole Lady Markbury's ruby necklace for her son to pay for the young swine's gaming debts and he then never saw a penny after he handed the necklace over, but how can you trust a blighter that robs his old Mum, I don't hold with that."

"Yes and who could he tell that he himself had been robbed" laughed Jem.

"His name was "Sam Jennings, poor devil, he got paid this time and no mistake by some rotter, gives us all a bad name that sort of thing, so we need to find who did it and set things straight."

"We will, you can be sure of that, and they had the cheek to kill him here in my domain and in My Lady's grounds, I am not having that," said Chalfont coldly with a nasty gleam in his eyes.

Meanwhile Shelly was giving her guests coffee she felt happier than she had felt for a long time. She could not explain it to herself. Later Archie and James were going to stroll with James's dog in the grounds, Hiram was planning to do a little snooping after another loving look at his cars. Charleen after looking at them with him planned to write some letters telling all her friends she was staying with a real English lady in a beautiful very old house.

Shelly told them after coffee she needed to get ready for

her new guests coming today.

"I only hope they are as nice as you all."

The Americans smiled at these words. "Well Lady Shelley if you are willing I have two more guests for you Dirk Montana my favourite leading man star who I will be starring in my next movie, you will like, him a swell fellow and all the ladies love him, and also my secretary Ruth Renner I would find her useful right now, a nice gal very quiet but good company to have around, that's if you have more room."

"Of course, we have plenty of rooms, I have not been to the movies for quite a while as I was in mourning but I know of Dirk Montana, who doesn't, I will tell Chalfont. Oh there you are, Can you have the extra rooms prepared?"

"Of course My lady, and also the police have arrived they are waiting in the hall."

"Please send them in, oh and also some coffee for them."

"Very well My Lady."

Chalfont gave his little bow and left.

"Say he's a great guy, a perfect butler, do you think he

would like to be in one of my movies?"

Shelly looked startled "I have no idea."

James was looking thoughtful, a handsome movie star was not in his opinion a good thing to have around, Archie only laughed and said "Chalfont in a movie what an idea , a hoot, but I can't see him doing it, here he is king, rules the other staff, he is as you might say a great leader."

Parsons the head parlour maid had been standing in the hallway and listening, she had quite forgotten why she was there when she heard the magic words Dirk Montana, she clutched her chest and nearly fainted, she was so excited, her favourite heart throb was actually coming to stay at the hall, she would be able to see him everyday, she must get her hair done, she lost no time in rushing back to the kitchens to impart her news her eyes shining before Chalfont could, but he had beaten her to it.

"Well well well" said Mrs. Barclay, "Very handsome he is to be sure, but as I always says handsome is as handsome does, and we will have the girls all of a flutter, best keep a watch on them, we don't want none of that nonsense goings on here."

Parsons walked in with a superior air, blast Chalfont she had wanted to bring the news, "Any tea in the pot Mrs. Barclay? Looks like we will have our work cut out with movie stars all over the place." She sniffed fooling none of them.

Inspector Riley lifted his cup of coffee that Chalfont handed him and sipped it, "We have discovered the identity of the victim, he was a petty thief called Samuel Jennings, he usually worked in London not sure why he was so far from his usual haunts but but we want to find out, it will give us a clue why and by who he was killed, so we would like to take another look round."

"Of course Inspector feel free, we will do all we can to assist you, I shall be welcoming my new guests, so if you need anything ask Chalfont he will help you."

Hiram was delighted with this and went to put on his warm coat, he intended to follow the inspector and other police officers and observe their methods closely he had already telephoned Dirk and Ruth who would be arriving tomorrow.

Archie, James and his dog went out for a walk, they made

sure they went off in a different direction, James was using his stick with his other hand shoved deep in his pocket, it was much colder today, both men were wearing hats, scarves and overcoats. The little spaniel was bounding ahead happily exploring, occasionally he gave a little woof of pleasure.

"Now look here James old chap, I think I know or have damn a good idea what that bounder was after, didn't take much notice at the time but Simon in his cups one night told me that his father had done some fabulously wealthy Maharaja chappie a great service and the prince chappie had forced upon him a positive heap of precious gems. I saw a couple of unbelievably huge emeralds, Simon let me see them and he said they were nothing, there were a lot more tucked away. Shelley has never mentioned it, if she even knows about them, but she is so hard up and so they must be well hidden somewhere here or it stands to reason she would have them and the poor little soul wouldn't be so worried. Simon also said the old lord moved them from time to time, he would not need them himself but kept them for Simon and Shelly, he always told Simon where they were."

"Yes but this is a jolly huge place to search, good thing we have a free hand to wander about without arousing suspicion." James frowned as he spoke then scuffed his stick into a tuft of grasses.

"You say Simon told you about them, and showed you a couple of gems so we know for sure they exist, pity we don't know who else knows about them, who else he told, I am willing to bet Shelly knew about them and is probably puzzled where they are, remember she was snooping about the other night well aware that a murder had been committed, she must have have had a reason for it, she is not the kind of girl to give up easily either from what I have seen of her. I feel sure she will have searched the house. What about Chalfont do you think he knew about them? The thief was down here looking for them now you have told me so I think we can be pretty sure about that. They, who ever they are will try again and she could be in danger, good thing I have my pistol here with me and I won't be afraid be afraid to use it. Nobody will touch a hair of her head."

Archie gave him a searching look.

"Good man you do that very thing, I think you are right about Shelley knowing about the jewels Simon or even her father might have told her, Simon would have for sure and now I remember she was always much better at keeping secrets than him. I don't think Chalfont knew about them after all old boy, not the sort of thing to tell one's butler about. Yes some other blighter will come back but this time we will be ready for them."

Chapter 13

Shelly was waiting in the drawing room for her next quests, a Mrs Hopkiss and her daughter Caroline. Mrs. Hopkiss was a wealthy merchant's widow who had ambition for her darling daughter to marry into society. She also vaguely knew Shelly's aunt through donating to charity but this had not given her access to move in the circles she wanted to. When she saw the advert Shelley had put in a newspaper she was very excited and read it out to Caroline, "For my darling this is how you get into society as an introduction to stay with a real lady and her friends, You shall have new clothes before we go, just think my love we will dine with them as fellow guests and we have to dress for that, and you just might meet a nice young man a future husband, Lady Shelly was always seen with the right sort of young men until her poor father's accident. I cannot remember when I felt so pleased," said this good woman. Mrs. Hopkiss was a rather plump woman with good skin and a great deal of expensively dyed red fluffy hair, being very wealthy she could indulge herself with lots of clothes and jewels, she loved rubies and wore a lot of them. Caroline was a very slim pretty red head, she had been sent to good schools and had lavish amounts of money spent on her by a doting mother. Her mother may give some the impression that she was a foolish woman but she was anything but, she was in fact a very shrewd woman.

"Very well Mums it might be fun, I shall need some new pearl clips and also some new evening slippers, all mine got scuffed."

"Of course my lovely. Get some new evening gowns too, a fur wrap and a nice pearl and diamond pin for your hair. Get all you the rest you need for a long stay at a country house party too."

"Welcome, said Shelly, greeting the two ladies, "I do hope your journey wasn't too tiresome, Parsons will show show you to your suite of rooms to freshen up and then we can have some tea afterwards."

"Thank you your Ladyship too kind I am sure." Mrs. Hopkiss was dressed in a purple travelling suit and hat, she had a lots of furs hanging from her shoulders. She shook hands with Shelly and wasn't sure if she should curtsey or not. Caroline was more at ease, she was wearing a mauve tweed coat and skirt, matching bag and shoes and had a velvet hat perfectly set on her red curls, she smiled and said "Thank you that would be wonderful."

They were shown up by Parsons and were delighted with the rooms that overlooked the gardens. Fires were burning brightly it looked very inviting. They took off their coats and hats, powdering noses and brushing hair before going down for a cup of welcome tea. They had a bedroom each that led into a private sitting room and a shared bathroom, their trunks and cases had been brought up and their own maidservant Gladys was busy unpacking and seeing to their clothes.

"You know my dear this is all very nice." Caroline wasn't really listening, putting her jacket back on to go downstairs she had seen through the windows two very handsome young men strolling back towards the house with a gambolling spaniel running beside them. She smiled Mums was going to be pleased. Then she saw two police constables stopping to speak to them she decided not to mention the police to her mother but find out what it meant herself. She was too late. Gladys squawked with sniff "There is policemen out there Madam, oh my gawd police."

Mrs. Hopkiss rushed to the windows "Whatever do you mean!" The constables had disappeared around the side of the house.

"I am sure it is nothing Mums they are probably doing it to keep an eye on things that's all."

"But why would they need to, that's what I want to know?" Caroline scowled at Gladys she knew very well the maid was not happy to be here away from her young man in Manchester. Gladys seeing the look quickly shut up.

"Mums all I saw were two very handsome young gentlemen just come back to the house and they seemed very relaxed and at home. They were laughing with the policemen so probably it's all about poachers" said Caroline with a meaningful look at her mother.

Mrs. Hopkiss was mollified and "No doubt her Ladyship will tell us all about it."

"Not over tea Mummy."

They went down to tea, Mrs. Hopkiss a little worried about the police sighting because she had brought all her jewels, well you never knew when you might need them and she liked to change them around. She had also just bought her daughter some fine pearls and a delicate diamond pendant.

Before they left their rooms Caroline said coldly "Mums Gladys is making a fuss about nothing she is acting a bit fed because she left her boyfriend behind."

"What! If she thinks to play up she can have her notice, and so I shall tell her and no mistake, this much more important than her boyfriend."

They smiled as they walked downstairs, a footman Jem showed them to the drawing room where Chalfont was bringing in some tea. Mrs. Hopkiss noticed James and Archie first and smiled to herself. Bother everything else this was the chance for her Caroline.

"Hello hello hello" Archie greeted them cheerfully. Shelley introduced everybody and they all sat down. They were surprised and delighted to meet a famous film producer. Soon Archie began talking to Caroline who he thought very pretty. Hiram began to tell Mrs. Hopkiss he was going to make a British murder mystery for his next film. She laughed and said "Oh so that's what we saw outside just now. My maidservant said she saw some police constables but silly girl I see now they were really only actors."

There was an awkward silence then Hiram answered her cheerfully "Oh no Ma'am they were the real thing, we had ourselves a real live murder."

Mrs. Hopkiss started and looked shocked but Archie seeing the way the wind was blowing laughed it off lightly saying "Some bally poacher don't you know, nothing for you to worry your pretty little heads about. and anyway you have all of us to look after you." He gave her his charming smile. She still looked doubtful so he added "Tomorrow Hiram here is bringing down the most famous film star in the world none other than Dirk Montana!"

Caroline gasped in delight and Mrs Hopkiss relaxed,it couldn't be dangerous if they were bringing famous film stars here. Shelley breathed a sigh of relief and silently blessed her old friend for saving the day.

"Please call me Lady Shelley all my friends do" she told them."
This pleased Mrs. Hopkiss to think of it, friends with a member of the nobility whatever would her Joe have thought of that, they had money of course from the factory and mill but this was what she had always wanted, she remembered her new evening gowns and her jewels with pride. She wouldn't worry. This was her Caroline's chance. "Call me Dolly, Lady Shelley, that's what my late husband used to call me, and my friends do now.

"We are all chums here. I hope you have all you need, ask

Chalfont if anything else is required, we have another guest coming down this afternoon a Major Grimshaw-Peake he is just returned from India he has retired and will be with us while he looks for a property to buy of his own."

"I say after lunch would you like to see over the grounds?" asked Archie, he looked at both women but smiled at Caroline.

Later after lunch Charleen and Dolly retired to their rooms for a rest, both ladies found warm fires burning and sat back in their comfortable arm chairs put their feet up and dozed off, the day had turned colder and neither lady intended going out getting their feet wet, they had a peaceful afternoon napping by their own fires ready for the evening.

Hiram went off to have a long peaceful loving look at his cars, he slowly walked around each one touching them lovingly and sitting in each of them, he sighed with pleasure.

Archie and Caroline walked briskly ahead of James and Shelly, they were all well wrapped up in coats hats and boots, although colder it was a dry sunny Autumn day, the slight breeze was blowing golden leaves around much to the delight of Toby the spaniel who had great fun chasing the leaves. Archie and Caroline were soon out of sight Archie was going to take her around the lake. James was happy to have Shelly to himself but sad too because he knew he could never win her, he scuffled some leaves for Toby with his stick and said crossly "This leg of mine is a damn nuisance slows me down."

"Really, it seems the right pace for me, I prefer to look at things and enjoy my walks not march them, You were wounded defending our country, a hero and you will get better. Don't try to rush things. Oh do look at that cheeky little robin he seems to be following us, I do love to see them."

James turned to her and saw her beautiful face, flushed by the cold her eyes sparkling with delight at everything around her, but he saw only her, and he was thinking of an answer, she means it he thought, she really thinks I am a hero, but the heroes were the ones who gave their lives and can never again come home to all this, they died for our freedom, I am one of the lucky ones. Before he could speak Jem did, he had come up behind them to tell Shelly the police inspector and sergeant hoped to see her again before they left.

"Bother!" said Shelly, "I was enjoying our walk so much, I suppose I shall have to go back to the house and see them." She bent to fuss Toby who adored her and turned to go back. James thought a much stronger word and one he would not utter in front of a lady. He said, "I am coming with you to find out what they know. Let's hope it's some good news."

Jem watched them as he followed them back to the house he smiled to himself, that James is sweet on her and no mistake he thought. He vowed to tell Chalfont, the Guv now, James was a good one he thought.

"Where did Chalfont park the police officers Jem?"
The library My Lady" answered Jem.

They got back to the house where Shelly removed her outer things and ran up to powder her nose, "Meet you in the library" she called to James. His man was there waiting to take his coat and the now tired Toby.,

Chalfont had quite rightly guessed what would happen, he seemed to have eyes everywhere and was keeping a close eye or in fact several pairs of eyes on his mistress.

"Good afternoon sir is Lady Sherringham with you?" asked Inspector Riley.

"Powdering her nose and will be here in a moment."

"Ah of course" said the Inspector with a smile, the three men exchanged looks as if to say women bless their hearts.

Just then Shelly came through the door, "I've sent for tea it's so jolly well cold outside," she informed them as she came in.

The three men turned to welcome her before they all sat down.

Jem had reported back to Chalfont saying "That James is sweet on Lady Shelly I can tell you that for sure."

"No harm in that, he's a good one, and also she will be safe outside with him around, the dog will soon let him know if there is any strangers and I happen to know from Treach that he carries a pistol."

"Cor! Yes she'll be safe enough alright."
Chalfont took the tea and so was able to hear what was happening.

"We will continue with our inquiries Lady Sherringham we

told you the name of the victim, there will be an inquest and I expect a murder by persons unknown verdict at the moment, we have no idea who murdered him because he usually works alone" said Inspector Riley taking a cup of tea from Chalfont.

"Looks like a case of thieves falling out" said Sergeant Mathers.

"We don't believe there is any danger to you or your guests, but we will be leaving a couple of constables to keep an eye on things just to be sure, you will see them around, we want them to make their presence felt, a warning if you will. I hope that won't be an inconvenience to you or your guests" the Inspector said with a smile.

"Oh no quite the opposite, Hiram will love it, and Mrs. Hopkiss will be happier" laughed Shelly.

"Ah yes we have already seen the gentleman in question and you have a famous film star coming tomorrow he tells me, with all the fuss that will generate you will certainly have your hands full."

"Yes we certainly will, lots of new guests I suspect will

want to come but we have all the ones we want when the last few arrive."

The two police officers shook hands with Shelly and James before Chalfont showed them out.

"As nice a lady as you could wish for" remarked Sergeant Mathers to his superior officer.

"Yes she is and I am glad she has such good loyal friends around her because I have a feeling that this is far from over, I wonder what our bird was after really, and don't say it was the cars because I won't believe it for a moment."

"I shouldn't say any such thing, he'd have a rare old job starting one of those up with that butler of hers, he's a downy one and no mistake, doesn't miss a thing."

"Yes I noticed that, but you are forgetting he wasn't here when it took place, away shopping for her Ladyship."

"That's true. He brought back some new help too and I have to say they look a bit familiar, can't quite put my finger on it but I have seen them before."

"I shouldn't wonder but I don't believe he'd play her false, one of those people that knows more than he is saying though, he has been with the family for years and she trusts him like her father did."

"Sad about that terrible accident."

"Hmmmn. Never been sure it was and I'm not the only one."

"Thank you James" Shelly was saying as Archie and Caroline came in.

"I say was that the police chaps again, did we miss all the fun?"

"Nothing else has happened has it?" asked Caroline. "What have we missed?"

"Oh no, there will be some constables staying on duty, just as a precaution, you may see them popping out of the bushes" James tried to make light of it catching Archie's eye though.

"There is nothing to worry about, please reassure your mother, the police are doing their job and still watching over us that's all.

It was unfortunate to have happened just before you

arrived but the Inspector thinks it was a petty thieves falling out and nothing more, he doesn't thank the other one will return and is off somewhere miles away, but he is of course still looking into it. The inquest is in a couple of days we don't need to attend and he isn't expecting anything to come of it so early in his inquiries."

Caroline said "I will tell my mother, and we will be staying." She smiled at Archie as she said it. The two men went off to play a game of billiards, they wanted to compare notes too. Caroline found her mother drowsily sitting with her feet up and comfortable in front of the fire. She told her mother about the police visit laughing and saying it was exciting.

"Well I don't think so, this is not what I expected, and so I tell you, the police have never had cause to come to our house."

"Oh Mums I don't think we need worry, I have been out with Archie, that was fun. He's a lamb, I really like him, and he is if I am not mistaken, entirely smitten. We should stay on here now, I need to get to know him better and that won't happen if we leave. He and Lady Shelley are like brother and sister she is interested in James, you see what I know now already, I do like Lady Shelley we are becoming friends."

Chapter 14

Mrs. Hopkiss brightened all police activities forgotten at this news "Well that's more like it you clever little puss, I knew we should come here, you are just as fine as any of them you went to the best schools money could buy, you can go anywhere fit in and no mistake, you look a picture in your clothes too, only the best for my girl. Now be a dear and ring for that Gladys to make some tea, I am that parched."

Caroline laughed she had won as she knew she would, Mums was such a snob.

The next guest arrived, Major Grimshaw-Peake drove

himself in his car and pulled up outside. He stretched after getting out of his car and took a long look round. "This will do nicely" he said to himself, "England at her finest, cool and green and everything I dreamed of coming home to." He was a tall man with a very military bearing, he had a deeply tanned leathery face of one who has spent a lot of time out in a very hot climate, he was slightly balding with fair whitish hair and a white clipped moustache. His deep blue eyes were sharp missing nothing. He went up the steps and rang the bell.

Chalfont answered the door directing Pete to park the Major's car while Jem took control of the Major's luggage.

"Lovely part of the world" said the Major in his deep gruff voice.

"Yes sir it is, I will take you to meet Lady Sherringham, she is seated in the drawing room."

Shelly put down the book she was reading and turned to meet him, she knew he was an old friend of her fathers, they had been apparently together in India although she herself had never met the major.

"Please don't get up on my account My Lady" he said gruffly, taking her hand, "It is a great pleasure to meet you at last, I spent sometime with your Father of course in India and we had been to school together many years ago. We were great chums in those far off days" He shook his head sadly "I was sorry to hear of his and young Simon's deaths, a bad business a very bad business." He sat on the chair she indicated and looked at her with his bright blue eyes.

"Thank you Major, most kind, it still seems unreal. May I offer you a cup of tea after your long drive, then Chalfont can show you to your room." .

"Thank you that would be most welcome. I understand you have some other guests already."

"Yes we do, it's quite a jolly party you will meet them all or rather the ones here already at dinner later." Before she could ring for tea Chalfont appeared with a laden tray.

"Ah!" the Major sighed. They spent a pleasant hour the Major telling her some amusing tales of her father and himself when they were boys, and later in India through being friends with

The Maharaja. Her father had invited him to visit Rosewood Hall when he returned to England he was very sad to have been too late to see his old friend. Shelly had enjoyed the stories, she then explained that he could explore the grounds, fish in the river and make himself feel at home.

"Of course you may meet some policemen but I am sure that won't bother you at all." She then explained the situation all over again. The Major looked thoughtful and tutted.
Shelly rang for Chalfont to show the old soldier his room.

"Dinner will be at eight" she said.
The Major smiled gave her a little salute.

"This way sir if you will follow me" said Chalfont,
Shelly sighed she was tired of explaining a corpse away, she wondered where James and Archie were and went in search of them.

Chapter 15

Shelly met Hiram in the hall, he had just come in and was on his way upstairs to see his wife, he told Shelly that Archie and James were out with the cars and had promised to lock up before they came in. Shelly dressed warmly in coat, hat and scarf and slipping on warm boots went to find them. She heard their voices as she got to the door and decided to play a prank on them. She slipped silently in through the doors and stopped to listen. Suddenly she was very interested and decided to keep quiet. They were over in the shadowy far corner looking at a pile of dusty crates, the crates were covered with old sacks and blankets and were filthy with dirt and oil. It was very dark in that part of the coach house.

"Hello what's this?" She heard James ask. He was bent down behind the crates, she knew what was there, her heart seemed to jump.

"Oh that was Simon's pet project, he had started building it, you know how he was always tinkering about with engines, he had the idea he wanted to build his very own motor car."

"He was doing a damn fine job too, he made a good start, it's a shame if it won't ever be finished " answered James.

Shelly knew what she must do.

Archie replied sadly "Yes, I remember him telling me all about it. It was something he loved working on, look there is his overall still hanging on the peg on the wall, damn it if I can still see him wearing it, hands all covered with grease and laughing."
Both men were silent for a moment. Shelly unknown to them blinked back tears. Suddenly she straightened herself determined that they would never know she had listened and heard them.

"I wondered where you had got to I should had guessed."

She smiled at them both.

"Hello old Thing," said Archie greeting her

"I see you have found Simon's car he was very fond of that, all the other bits are in the crates, they have not even been opened."

"I can see he had done quite a bit" said James quietly, with his shy smile, he was leaning against the wall now wearily, remembering how Simon and he talking engines and their love of tinkering with them, and also other friends who shared that love gone forever in the war. He sighed and went to straighten himself, but slipped on some oil, he grabbed at the overalls to save himself from falling and as they moved he said "Hello what's this." There was a piece of dirty sacking sticking out of a deep sort of crack in the wall, it had been hidden by the overalls hanging on their hook on the wall.

James thinking it was an odd thing to find so put his hand out and pulled at the sacking, it came out with a whoosh and was unexpectedly heavy, he dropped it in surprise and it fell to the floor with a muffled metallic clang. They all three leant forward to see what it was. The sacking had slipped partly revealing a heavy wrench.

"I say James old boy what the devil is this?"

"Don't touch it, I think we just found the murder weapon." There was a darker stain on one end only just visible.

"How horrid," whispered Shelly with a shiver.

"That proves he was killed in here but why move the body.?"

"Let's go back to the house" said James giving him a meaningful look.

"Of course" he answered quickly. "You go on and I will lock up."

Shelly shivered "Can we keep this to ourselves tonight? It isn't going to make any difference to the poor man who was killed after all, and I would prefer not to upset our guests again tonight or Mrs. Hopkiss might leave right away."

"Rather. We lock up here and ring the police in the morning" agreed Archie.

"I rather like them, Dolly and Caroline" said Shelly as they went back to the door.

"So do I" agreed Archie with a grin.

"How was the Major?" asked James trying to keep lightening the mood.

"He's rather a dear, and talked about being friends with my father and fun they had. I enjoyed hearing about them."

Archie carefully locked the doors and they made their way thoughtfully back to the house. Unseen by them Pete came out to double check the doors were safely locked. Chalfont was keeping a very close watch on things.

Shelly went off to her rooms she was feeling a little shaken finding the murder weapon it was awful to think somebody had killed a man in part of her home, she shivered and was glad to sit down by the warm fire in her private sitting room, her cats immediately jumped up onto her lap and began purring lovingly, she bent her head to them so glad of their company, she sighed and thought how lucky she was to have James and Archie staying here too. She wondered again what had happened to the jewels her Father and Simon had hidden, they were hers now and she had searched everywhere for them but the old house was huge with many nooks and corners, if the murder victim had been looking for them too and she was sure he was,, who had told him about them? Were they in fact buried in the grounds somewhere?

That was possible and would be a huge task to find them out there. She had walked around looking for a likely spot but had no idea where they could be,, but that she supposed was the idea of a hiding place. It gave her hope that they were still here somewhere. She was determined to find them, she already knew where they were not. Shelly thought I shall have to search Daddy's and Simon's rooms again it had been too painful before, although she had braced herself and done it before locking their rooms up and keeping the keys here in her own rooms. Next time I will think about getting James and Archie to help me she thought. James would think like Simon she could see why they were friends. Could she really impose though, he was supposed to be resting. It wasn't she didn't trust her servants she just hadn't been able to bear anyone to go into the rooms and disturb their things, she could not explain to herself why.

She thought I will also ask James to finish Simon's car, it really should be done and I could see he loved it as much as Simon did, I understand why they were friends, Archie would hate getting all dirty and oily, James would enjoy doing it and it would take his mind off his bad leg while it gets better, if we hadn't found that awful weapon thing I would have suggested it then. Of course he may not want to and refuse but somehow I don't think so. She began to feel sleepy from the warmth of the fire and the soothing purrs. She dozed off.

Archie went up with James to his rooms for a snifter and a chat.

"So what do you think about the Major?" asked James when they were seated on either side of the fire sipping a brandy each. "I ask because it seems a bit rummy him turning up now suddenly, if he had been such a pal of Lord Sherringham why didn't he visit before? Why didn't he come to the funeral? He told Shelly he spent time with her father in India and was a pal of the Maharaja too, so it stands to reason if true he would have known all about whatever it was Lord Sherringham and Simon did, and also how they got rewarded."

"Yes I agree it is rummy, I do know they knew a major out there but I don't remember his name. He may be the genuine article. I agree he would know all about Simon and Lord Sherringham's little escapade or possibly escapades out there and that is more likely, they got up to some things I can tell you always seemed to live for adventures and excitement, but what I can't tell you is what that particular one was. It was a always a secret so I can't test him on it, already thought that one out, and here's the thing, I doubt if Shelly knows either, I mean to say might have been a bit personal don't you know. We keep a close eye on him watch him like a bally hawk. We watch him and listen to what he says at dinner tonight ."

"Yes but he will be being careful if he's up to no good."

"If the blighter starts poking around where he shouldn't we will be waiting."

Chalfont in fact had his own plans.

Shelly had dressed carefully in a dark blue silk gown and a rather exotic lapis and diamond set a gift from her father. She went

went down to find Hiram waiting by himself he explained Charleen was still fussing with her dressing and he had escaped, she laughed, she liked the big American and offered him a drink. "I am glad you are down first I did want a quiet word with you, but this is secret for as long as possible."

"OK . Lady Shelly you can count on me."

"Thank you Hiram I knew I could." She told him of the events and find in coach house. "I will report it in the morning to the police, until they have been and investigated again we all have to stay out of there, I really am so sorry I know how much you love visiting your cars."

Hiram whistled softly "I understand I truly do, I guess somebody is going to be in real trouble for missing finding that thing. Tomorrow Dirk and Ruth will be here so I will have those guys to deal with, I sure was looking forward to showing them my new babies but you don't need to bother none about me and Charleen, we will do just fine, she is having a grand old time and I look forward to meeting the Inspector and Sergeant again."

Shelly laughed "That's why I told you, but the thing is

James found it by accident it was hidden in the very wall itself very hard to find, you wouldn't have seen it if you were looking, he sort of fell against it." She looked thoughtful something made her think again about her own words.

"Still I am thinking somebody will be in for it."
The other guests started coming down and so they changed the subject.

Later Archie whispered in her ear "Hiram."

"I already dealt with it" she said smugly and smiled.

"Dinner is served My Lady" said Chalfont."
After dinner the men who wanted to went out and smoked in the garden then retired to the drawing room where Chalfont had brought in coffee, it was warm, everyone seemed relaxed. Charleen and Dolly were both wearing some impressive sparkling jewels but Shelly had her pendant admired. Caroline wore her new pearls, all the ladies were beautifully gowned and made a pretty picture sitting and talking happily to each other. Dolly thought this is what I have always wanted for my girl nothing is too good for her, murder or not we are staying, I have eyes in my head and I can see

the way that Archie looks at her and him a friend of Lady Shelly, why he practically has the run of the place too, she treats him like a brother so no problems there that I can see, he's no fortune hunter as far as I can tell. He can take my girl anywhere in high society open any doors for her, I must find out more about him. She looked across with satisfaction to where Archie sat talking to Caroline, they looked happy and were laughing together.

James and Archie were also watching the Major and encouraged him to talk about India, he was happy to do so and began to tell tales of adventures some with Lord Sherringham. He painted word pictures of bright colours, strange exotic lands, spices and music, hot sunshine and monsoon seasons, he told them he had only recently returned and found out his old friend was dead.

"I had always planned to come home to retire, often dreamed of my own place in the dear old country, Lord Sherringham had told me about the countryside around these parts and said it would be just the thing for me. So now I am here having met his charming daughter at last and do intend to look for a little place of my own. I shall miss my old friend." He gave a sad little smile. He said a lot but nothing either, that was proof enough for Archie and James.

James was sitting next to Shelly and watching the Major carefully.

There was one person who was really fascinated by the Major's story and asked him lots of questions and that was Mrs Dolly Hopkiss.

"Well I never did, I have never heard of such things, it all sounds so foreign. I feel like I've seen it myself now the way you tell it."

He turned to her and smiled she was the kind of woman he admired, a well rounded figure pretty and feminine. A fine looking woman, soft and kind. He liked the way she dressed too, bright and cheerful.

"Dear lady, tomorrow I shall begin to hunt for a house, a woman's advice on such things would be invaluable do you see, I am but a simple old soldier and beg you most humbly to help me out. I have two houses to inspect and ask you to come along and look them over, you will of course be able to point out any faults that an old duffer would miss."

She was surprised but delighted "Old duffer indeed! Of course I should be glad to come along it's true a woman can see things a man won't, and you can tell me some more of your wonderful adventure stories."

I bet he will thought Archie.

"Delighted dear lady and perhaps we can get a spot of lunch between viewings.

Dolly smiled her cheeks were pink with delight and Caroline saw this but she knew her mother was smart enough to spot any fortune hunters and so she was glad to see her enjoying herself. It will be good for her she thought He's rather an old darling.

They all had a pleasant evening chatting with each other in the warm comfortable room well pleased to be there together.

Chapter 16

The next morning was another lovely golden day but it had turned colder. Shelly waited until after breakfast and watched Dolly and the Major drive away before she phoned the police inspector. It was going to be a busy day.

Dolly had dressed with care much to Caroline's delight and Gladys sniffed until Dolly told her off.

"Give over do, as if I need that gloomy face first thing in the morning, fair sets the day off all wrong and I won't be having it". The widow was wearing a cherry coloured coat and a matching velvet scarf trimmed with black lace draped over her shoulders, her matching hat was trimmed with the same lace forming a sort of semi veil and black feathers, she looked like a woman going out and determined to enjoy herself. At last happy she was looking her best she picked up her bag and trotted down to where the gallant Major was waiting for her, she took his offered arm and they went out to his car.

Shelly sighed with relief, the major told her cheerfully they would be gone for several hours and not to expect them for lunch, Much as she liked both of them seeing the police without them would be easier, she made her phone call.

Inspector Riley and Sergeant Mathers soon arrived and after talking to Shelly followed Archie and James to the coach house, the Inspector looking grave and Mathers tutting quietly. James pointed to the half covered wrench still on the floor where he had dropped it, it could be easily seen now they knew where to look although it was very dark in this corner. The dirty sacking was hanging off. Sergeant Mathers wearing gloves picked it up carefully by the sacking covered end and handed it to Inspector Riley who was also wearing gloves. They carried it over to the open door.

"Looks like blood to me sir."

"That's almost certainly the case it will have to be sent off to be tested to be sure. You are sure you didn't touch it either of you?" He placed the heavy wrench into a clean sack to carry it.

Archie shook his head and James admitted to grabbing the sacking.

"I pulled it out of the wall when I saw sacking sticking out, don't even know why was just curious, only touched the sacking though before I dropped it, surprised because the thing was so heavy. I was also wearing gloves, been walking my dog and it was a coldish day."

"That's something I suppose" grumbled the Sergeant.

"Those constables should not have missed it, this is the murder weapon and that you two found it, something they should have, I shall be having a talk to them later" said the Inspector angrily.

"It wasn't an easy thing to spot I only found it by accident, I slipped on some greasy spot on the floor and reached out to save myself. My hand caught the sacking and I grabbed it to save myself, it was lodged in firmly and hidden behind some old overalls hung on a peg. Very dark over in that corner too." James knew the constables were in for it later, he had done his best for them. They should have found it but then they themselves didn't when they were looking around for clues.

They didn't realize that Jem and Pete had discovered it earlier and in fact left it sticking out on Chalfont's instructions.

"You have better show us exactly where this took place sir" said the Sergeant.

"Why were you over in that corner if I may ask out of interest?" Inspector Riley asked Archie as they made their way back over to the corner.

"We were looking at a car Simon, Shelly's brother had been building, he was a clever chap don't you know, always happiest when mucking about with motors of one sort or another, James was interested to see it so I took him when I thought Shelly was busy, painful memories and all that. We were busy talking when she came to find us and the rest happened as we told you."

"I see, you have known her Ladyship for a long time I understand."

"Practically since a tiny chick, we grew up together, spent most of my childhood with her and Simon, here at the hall."

"Our pater's were friends and I had lost my mother, don't even remember her, Shelly's mother was very sweet and kind and she looked after me like I was one of her own, we were all, well I mean to say, devastated when she died too. She was a great lady, Lord Sherringham was strange old stick, a good man who didn't bother us and we rather ran wild when away from school." Archie stopped suddenly " Sorry I ran on for a bit, of no interest to you." Inspector Riley didn't agree.

James was pointing to the spot where the overalls still hung, he stood back to let the Inspector through, it was a bit, narrow because of the half made car and the piles of crates. Sergeant Mathers pulled the overalls down and laid them carefully on top of one of the crates, they glanced at them they were covered with undisturbed thick dust and still tightly sealed fastened down with nails. The Sergeant sneezed. The Inspector was holding a light as well as the sack. Sergeant Matters drew a sketch in his note book before poking about in the crack in the wall, there was nothing more to be found, the old wall here was dark dusty and crumbling where he poked it, it was unlike the other end where the walls were clean and white washed showing the cars off in all their glory. The floor here to was dusty but churned up with footprints, not much use to them now, with the light's help they could see the grease spot and also it looked like dried blood possibly too. Sergeant Matther's scraped some of it up and put it in a jar. There was a smell of oil and dust everywhere.

"What I want to know is if chummy was killed here why go to all the bother to move the body. This is a dark spot not going to find a corpse too quickly anyway in this cold weather" he said.

Archie said "The way I see it is whoever did it, didn't want the body found immediately, for some other reason entirely. An alibi perhaps? Also they must have known about the impending car auction"

James answered. "Did we mention that?"

"You're right because although the coach house is usually

locked and not disturbed much, that changed everything" said Archie excitedly.

"Leave that all up to us sir" replied the Inspector firmly he was still furious with his men for not finding the weapon.

"We will lock up again and ask you to refrain from coming back in here until we have made another more thorough this time search. You locked up yourselves last night and nobody else came in?"

"As far as we know, and I can't think why anyone would on a cold dark night, the guests keep their cars in the old barn on the other side and also nobody went out."

In fact Chalfont, Jem and Pete had done so, they had found the weapon and made their own minds up also agreed with James and Archie why the victim had been moved. The boat house was a fare distance from the main house and who would want to visit it in the cold damp weather.

Chalfont had said "The killer didn't know about the coming guests whoever is behind this thought her Ladyship would be on her own."

"Yes that makes sense."

"Any ideas who?"

"Not yet but we are on the right track."

They didn't touch the weapon didn't need to just eased it a little sticking out of the wall and other prints they left didn't matter after all because they worked here and moved about freely.

Archie asked Inspector Riley "Are you coming to the house?"

"In a few minutes."

James and Archie watched the two senior officers walk off searching for the constables, they knew when they were found and could hear them getting ticked off by a furious Inspector. Archie and James discreetly went back to the house.

A few minutes later Inspector Riley and Sergeant Mathers were shown in where they had a few words with Shelly apologising to her explaining the situation and refusing the offer of coffee this time before they left. Archie told her the constables had been in trouble and made her giggle.

Archie went off in search of Caroline to bring her down for

coffee. James was left with Shelly in the library she turned to smile at him, she liked his quiet ways and shy smile that he now gave her.

"You were impressed by the car Simon had begun to build, it makes me feel sad to think it's just a pile of broken bits, such a waste never to be finished as he had planned. He loved it you see."

"Oh it's much more than that, a pile of bits I mean, he had done a lot, it could be finished with the rest of the parts although I didn't see any."

She saw the light in his eyes as he spoke just as she had expected, this sad wounded gentle man, she must play this carefully, Shelly was a clever woman and she had grown up with two men who looked like that when they spoke about engines, she also knew how to get her own way with them, she had thought about this a lot and had a plan of her own.

"James I believe the rest of the parts of the car are in those crates that are by the bit that has been made, I know it's off limits at the moment of course but you know as much about that sort of thing as Simon did, if you would find it fun to do you are welcome to finish building it, I feel very sure Simon would have wanted that, you were his friend."

James looked taken aback, he certainly liked the idea, he would enjoy working on the car and to finish it for her, she looked so sad when she spoke of Simon, it was something he would love too. He hadn't even thought about it until then. Shelly had, and also intended to give him the car too but that would be later.

"Of course Lady Shelly I would love to do it for you as long as the parts are all there." He grinned at her in a way that made her feel happy for some reason.

"Oh pooh!" she laughed. "Just Shelly we are good friends now. I am so glad, you are happy with the idea, I didn't know what to do with it and it would make me sad to leave it like that gathering dust."

Before James could answer Chalfont came in and said "My Lady some of the guests are in the drawing room shall I serve coffee there now, and would you like yours here?"

"No we are going to join them and coffee will be welcome."

James thought darkly perhaps it is for the best, but I really enjoyed having her here all to myself and close. He longed to hold and comfort her.

They were drinking coffee when the sound of new arrivals pulled up at the front door.

"Aha I think that will be Dirk" exclaimed Hiram cheerfully. Charleen smiled. They went to meet the famous star not all were happy to do so. The saw a really beautiful looking man with black wavy hair and a perfect profile that he showed off when getting out of the car and looking around. Hiram had sent his car to the station to meet him. He was tall, over six feet, slim and beautifully dressed, then he turned to face them, and strolled over to them he took Shelly's hand and gave her his famous boyish smile that had made so many female hearts beat a little faster, she saw those brilliant shining dark blue eyes, he had a way that made any woman he was with feel that she was the only woman in the world to him. She was caught in his charm and understood why he was the number one leading male film star in the world.

Chapter 17

"Thank you My Lady for inviting me to your beautiful home" he said in his deep seductive voice. He had in fact been grumbling all the way down on the train to his travelling companion Ruth Renner who had ignored him, she knew him too well. She sighed inwardly now in disgust. He had not wanted to leave London where he had been spending a lot of time with a beautiful merry widow with a shady reputation.

She had used him by inviting him to almost nightly parties where people fought for invitations to spent time with him, there were rumours of drugs being sold at them. Ruth had secretly sent a message to Hiram, who fearing a scandal and alarmed, sent for them, he needed to stop his hot property Dirk getting caught up in it. Seeing Dirk now you would never have guessed he had not been delighted to be here. Hiram noticed the dark shadows under Dirk's eyes and knew he had done the right thing.

Hiram greeted him and Ruth with delight and seeming unconcern.

Lunch was a merry affair the maidservants all dewy eyed and telling each other in the kitchen how the famous star had smiled at them. Mrs. Barclay got cross and said "Give over do and get on with your work, as if he would be interested in the likes of any of us. He won't be impressed with the service here if you keep looking at him with cow eyes, remember he is used to silly girls mooning about over him."

Chalfont agreed sternly. "Remember your places we will be having none of that here."

After lunch Hiram took Dirk off to show him around and tell him about his new film idea, he did not mention he had heard what Dirk had been up too but noticing again the dark shadows under his eyes he decided to watch him carefully, that broad in

London was bad news. Thank goodness for Ruth.

Ruth was busy unpacking in her room, she had liked Shelly immediately and she was happy to be here, glad Dirk was Hiram's problem now.

Dirk was looking around the grounds and looked back towards the hall he whistled "Quite a pile, and she is a mighty pretty girl."

Hiram was watching Dirk intently he saw that his good looking leading man was beginning to show some lines at the corners of his eyes and at the sides of his rather sulky mouth, not a real problem yet but he needed checking, his wild ways were not helping but he was still a big box office draw at the moment however that could change if any whiff of scandal got out, about him. He remembered back when one of his talent scouts told him about a potential find who was working waiting tables, he went to look for himself and "discovered" Dirk Montana or rather Maurice Shaunassy, a young Irishman, he took the young waiter and turned him into a star. He had been a natural, had all the looks, charm and talent needed, the camera loved him and very soon so did the film watching fans. He had been so grateful for the break and acted the part always until lately, maybe he knew himself he would slowly lose his handsome looks. Hiram still thought Dirk could go on for a few years yet if he took care of himself. He's a good actor but a fool to himself Hiram thought.

"Forget it" said Hiram but kindly. "Lady Shelly is broke, hell why do you think she is letting us stay here? I am paying that's what. Don't go messing with her she has folks looking out for her that wouldn't take kindly to it. You'd need a hell of a lot of bucks to keep up this place too if you really meant it, besides I really like her, don't make her fall for you unless you do mean it, she made me and Charleen real welcome and Charleen is having the time of her life here staying with the swells, don't say nothing now but she has been real sick she had that darn flu a while back and still needs to take it a might easy. Even with this weather here the change is doing her good. She is resting up a lot. She likes Lady Shelly too. Now why I called you down I have me a notion to make this British mystery film, a classy murder piece, we are going to film some of it over here and some back in the studios, you got the starring role, goes without saying, some high class British dick as I see it. Maybe a lord. I brought Ruth down to write the scripts, I am putting it together still at the moment. Now you know there has been a murder here, never mind that though, we are doing a high society story and I want you to soak it up a perfect opportunity, the important thing is we get to watch British cops working, they call them rozzers here and they do things differently. I want you to get the feel of the place, you are going to play a British guy so pal up with Archie and James, and that is another reason not to mess with Lady Shelly, I want you to learn that kind of British accent, a real high class one. This film is going to be big, really big, different from anything you have done before, but we got to get it right, you can do this."

  Dirk began to feel excited, he was surprised to hear Lady Shelly was broke and had thought they were just guests who had been invited to stay, not paying for their time here. His face had shown his interest in the new film idea and Hiram had noticed and decided to push the whole thing home.

  "It will do you good to be here too, the air is clean and the pace is slower, Charleen is improving all the time since we got here, you are also looking tired some, you need some of this fresh clean air, some exercise in these swell surroundings, some early nights too. It is important for us all to stay here, so put on that old charm and play nice."

For a moment Dirk looked a trifle sulky but he was fond of Charleen she had always been kind to him, had encouraged him to believe in himself when he was starting out and unsure of himself he owed her and besides he wanted this new part badly, he was smart enough to realise he needed to change styles he couldn't keep up with the fast action pace much longer and he knew of several younger up and coming actors who would jump at the chance, he knew his face was his fortune and knew he needed to take care of himself. Yes London had got stale with that woman becoming clingy. He wouldn't miss her. He had thought Ruth had been sent to drag him down here on a leash but now it seemed he was wrong, this was all good stuff. Hiram had been clever although Dirk didn't know it.

He laughed "You got it boss, I'm in, I like the sound of it

all. I'll do it right." Hiram slapped him on the back .

Charleen was having her usual afternoon nap in her rooms all cosy and contented. She was feeling better for having them. James and Archie went to James's set of rooms mainly to grumble about Dirk, they were not impressed seeing his effect on the girls. Shelly and Caroline had taken Toby for a walk in the garden and said they would be back soon.

"I wonder how Mum's is getting on with her Major? I hope she is enjoying herself, I think she was really looking forward to looking over the houses with him, it's the kind of thing she would like."

"Yes and he is a sweetie and will take care of her, it must be quite strange for him being back in England, he was hoping to move here to be near my father they were old chums."
The girls were becoming friends and enjoyed each others company, Toby was bounding about in the garden happily chasing shadows and thrown sticks..

They went back because the weather was getting chilly, Treach took Toby and dried his wet feet before taking him back to his master.

Chapter 18

The girls went to the drawing room where Shelly rang for tea. The were soon joined by Archie and James who knew they were back when Treach had deposited a sleepy dog back to James's rooms Toby curled up on the rug before the fire and began to snore softly.

Archie and James were not so happy when Hiram and Dirk joined them, they liked Hiram but were wary of the famous handsome film star, but then although Dirk was very pleasant to Shelly and Caroline he sat closer to them, and asked them about a game or two of billiards later that evening. He and Hiram had some tea with them but did not stay long saying they needed to talk about the scripts in Dirk's rooms. Dirk asked them some questions about the countryside and although they didn't know it he was listening to their speech and accents very carefully. He was determined to befriend them and had soon seen that Archie was smitten with Caroline and he was faintly annoyed about it working out that she was very wealthy as well as pretty, but he decided it wasn't a good idea to try his charm or romance her after all, it would cause trouble with Hiram and he needed this film badly he was really excited about it too, It was something new for him, instead told them he was dying to see the collection of cars, the talk became about motor cars just all boys together, Shelly and Caroline looked at each other knowingly and smiled.

    The two Americans went upstairs and James soon followed going up to his own rooms to rest before the evening, he was getting better he knew, but needed some painkilling medicine his Doctor had given him and a sleep as ordered by that worthy man who had known James as a child. Caroline left after a while too saying it would be nice to have the suite to herself without Mums for a while and a long hot bath. Archie watched her go and Shelly giggled.

"You're stuck with me my old Chum, and that's that. . I do like your friend James he is very quiet and sad, don't worry I won't fuss over him I know he would hate it, do you think he will get better? I can see he is in pain. If you know of anything I can do, please do tell me. It is the least we can do for our heroes."

"Don't pity him old girl or he will be off like a shot, that's why he left his own home, too much of the fussing over him, so don't do it. I still remember that injured bird you found and took up to the nursery, putting the thing into a dolls cot without anyone knowing, I can still hear the nurses screams when she found it dead, and didn't you throw a paddy when Chalfont himself came to bury it, he helped you have a funeral to stop the tears."

"Darling Chalfont I don't know what I would do without him, he has always taken such good care of us. Oh Archie why did this all have to happen? We used to have so much fun I mean without dead things."

Archie put his arm around her patting her back gently, he

loved her like a sister, he could see her blink back tears he missed Simon too.

"I know old thing, that's the way it goes sometimes, a bad show I agree, but I am glad you aren't engaged to that bounder any more. I thought I might have to call him out."

She laughed, "I have no idea why I did it, it all seemed to be happening to somebody else, I didn't even like him."

Archie stared at her in amazement "Didn't even like him! Really Shelly! Well if that doesn't beat all."

"You like Caroline don't you, don't worry your secret is safe with me my dearest Archie."

"I should say I jolly well do, I think she is the one girl in the world for me, I'd like to marry her but she is so jolly well rich don't you know, and her mother might think that's why I am asking her. It's not though Shelly, she is different from most girls I meet, she's a topper, her smile, her laugh, the way her eyes sparkle, and the way she makes me feel being with her, A spiffing girl do you see?" he said earnestly.

"Archie it sounds like you have it bad, the real thing, I have never felt like that about anyone and have decided never to marry. Blow how rich she is. You should tell her how you feel, if she feels the same way what does it matter what anyone else thinks, just be happy."

"That is easy to say, but I couldn't do it, what if she laughs or turns away in disgust?" he said sadly.

"Don't be silly you goose, she is not the kind of girl to laugh, I like her, I don't know how she feels about you, I don't know her well enough to be able to tell but I do know this she will be able to tell a real fortune hunter from someone who is genuine about caring for her, if you really care then make her happy, and besides do you want somebody else to marry her. Dirk for instance? Do you know I once though of marrying you, I was going to ask you, had it all planned what to say too. I thought we would be comfortable with each other as we know each other so well and get on." Archie paled at both thoughts she had stirred him deeply.

"Dash it Shelly, you little beast, I love you like a sister but comfortable? Not exactly what a chap wants to hear. No I wouldn't like to see her with anybody else. Are you thinking of falling for the Dirk star next?"

She laughed "No silly not a bit, he is very handsome it's true but I would never be sure if he were trying out his lines on me or really meaning what he said. Sadly I shall always be alone. I will take up good works and boss people about "

He looked relieved as they laughed together, his Shelly was safe from film stars and fortune hunters and he owed it to Simon to keep it that way.

Major Grimshaw-Peake and Dolly Hopkiss were enjoying themselves very much,they really liked each other's company. The first house they had looked at was a beautiful old manor built of pale stone,it was warm and welcoming. Dolly fell for it immediately and decided if things didn't work out the way she was hoping and John as he told her to call him didn't buy it she would herself,she was tired of living in a city now she was here in the countryside, and she saw herself having weekend house parties for a few select friends,she included Shelly and James now,also she had high hopes for Archie becoming her son in law. The old house was in good order, the butler and his wife who was housekeeper showed them around. She loved all of it the soft mellow rooms, windows looking out at pretty but overgrown gardens,and began making plans,The Major watched her fondly. He asked the servants if they wanted to stay on. "Oh yes sir, we do most definitely, if we can" they answered quickly. "The old squire passed on a year ago and we have taken good care of the manor."

"Indeed you have."

After that John and Dolly looked around the second house, Dolly was quiet, this one was not for her,she had to wait and see what John decided to do. she sighed.

"Are you tired my dear? Let's have lunch,I know of the perfect place."

Dolly was thinking of the old yellow stoned manor house or she might have wondered how he had known of a perfect place to have lunch here.

They were soon seated in a private parlour in a pretty old inn. A log was burning brightly in the huge fireplace.They were very happy to be together it felt like they had known each other for a long long time.

  Dolly spoke first "John,it has been a while since I have enjoyed an outing like this,thank you for allowing me to see the houses."

  "You like the first one don't you, Croft Manor?" he said softly.

  "Yes and to be really honest I could see myself being happy living there,oh dear that came out wrong, dear me, it's your choice of course,please take no notice." She had turned quite pink,flustered she took a hasty sip of wine.

  "My dear of course I am taking notice of you, I am just a simple old soldier,not much of a ladies man never have been,I have not looked forward to spending my last years alone,I always was busy surrounded by other people,it is sudden I know but you and I could be very happy together,at our age why should we wait when we don't have to, Dolly my dear,I am not doing very well at this pray forgive me, I can only say I can see you gracing that beautiful house, dare I hope, Dolly dear sweet lady would you make a lonely old soldier happy, become my wife and share our lives there together?"

The Major was looking at her,she put her wine down carefully with a shaking hand and slipped her plump little hand in his.

"Oh yes John, I need no time to make up my mind,I will marry you,we will be happy making that lovely old place our home,I know we will do very well together,I ask only that we keep it secret for a little while, I can see our youngsters are shaping up to make a match of it,hopefully two, so let us let them sort themselves first,then we will have our own time,and you have made me so very happy." She dabbed her eyes and smiled, pink with pleasure.

He took both her hands and kissed them, then her mouth. She giggled girlishly . He ordered a bottle of champagne," I feel wonderfully wicked"she giggled again.

"I am so happy my dear,your wishes are my commands,we shall be blissfully happy, you will be the light of my life. We may need to give them a little nudge, I will in the meantime go ahead and buy the manor."

She said "Yes Archie follows Caroline around like a puppy dog,I can't understand why he hasn't proposed,a little nudge may be needed. We can have a quiet wedding,oh my goodness,I had thought myself to be alone forever and now this,it is wonderful,we will be such good company for each other." She smiled at him as they held hands and supped champagne.

He beamed at her, "We will still appear to be looking at other houses it gives us a good excuse to be off out together,It will be nice to spend time and we can plan what we are going to do."

"I feel very excited in a way I never believed,we can go back and visit our new home too,and plan how we will make it our own."

"Of course Dolly my dear,we will go there whenever you choose, I will cancel the other house visits and you can plan as much as you want,we can ask the butler about a gardener I have always wanted to grow roses and now I have a lady to give them too."

Chapter 19

The film star in question after spending time with Hiram had gone up to his room, and was standing looking out of a window across the park, he had a glass of Scotch whiskey in his hand and he was feeling very tired, his time in London had taken it's toll. Eugenie if that was even her name, she was a French woman of easy morals she had quickly and easily become his mistress but that was nothing new, he was used to women throwing themselves at him it was all part of the fame game, he had suspected her parties were a way of her earning an unlawful but rich living and he made sure she did not trap him, she used him cleverly but then he had shared her bed, he would not miss her in the least she had been fun for a while but he had escaped now here. He liked here, so relaxed and he needed a rest and now this great break, a new film to star in and an exciting one at that, he would clean up his act. Become a British gentleman detective. Hiram was watching him but he wanted to do it for his own sake, he would throw himself into the role and show the world just what he could do, he felt good.. Just then came a gentle tap on the door, he put down his glass and turned slowly just as the door opened, a pertly pretty maidservant called Maude stepped into the room she had come to make up the fire and she got the full force of his famous perfect profile, she gasped and nearly dropped her coal heavy scuttle.

"So sorry sir," she stammered trying to bob a curtsy while carrying the coal scuttle "I didn't know you was in here." She had blushed scarlet and said " I brought you some more coal to keep your fire burning so it don't go out, I can come back later otherwise."

She was a very pretty blonde fresh faced girl Dirk noticed,

and under his breath he said to himself "Oh I would very much like you to come back later and keep my fire burning" but instead, he like he had done in so many of his films strode across the room in a very tough and masculine way.

He with a smile took the scuttle from her startled hands and carried it to the fireplace for her, giving her another of his devastating smiles, she nearly swooned as he brushed against her.

"I am afraid I not much use with these here fireplaces coming from Hollywood like I do" he told her in his deep seductive voice, he was well aware of the effect he was having on her. He gave her another smile like they were sharing a secret. She was caught like a rabbit in headlights for a minute or two.

"Oh no sir let me do that" she rushed across and stood so close to him she touched him, he had put the scuttle in the hearth, he stepped back and watched her kneel and put coals on his fire, a pretty sight and he enjoyed it but he wanted the film more.

Maude went back to the kitchen in an excited state full of all that had happened, she had met her idol and he was just as she had dreamed about..

"Ooh just fancy" she gasped dancing in excitement "I've watched him many a time on the films, but now I met him stood so close he touched me, I don't want to ever wash again, he smiled at me, really at me like I saw him do at Sharon Starr in Time Will Tell, and he is ever so much a gentleman come straight over and took the scuttle touching my hands, and then he carried it for me, me, I swear I nearly swooned, came over ever so faint I did." Jem scowled menacingly "He touched you, what do you mean by that." They had become close and he had hopes.

"Not like that silly, what do you take me for. I told you he was a real gentleman."

The other maidservants all started talking at once until Mrs Barclay banged her rolling pin on the table, "Enough of this foolishness, you are a silly girl Maude and no mistake, do you really think he would take notice of a girl like you when he has all them glamour puss film stars around him all the time, not to mention Her Ladyship, you don't go back up to his room again, annoying her Ladyship's guests with silly swooning and such like, I never heard anything like it and I won't stand for it. Letting us all down, such goings on, I have no patience with it."

"I never did anything" began Maude sulkily as another maid pinched her angrily.

Chalfont spoke sternly " Enough! In future only one of the male staff will go to his rooms, I think it's best and no more of this nonsense, disturbing the peace here. Not another word about it. It will soon be time to serve one of your excellent teas Mrs Barclay, for our lucky guests."

The maidservants sighed and glared at Maude, "Trust you" they muttered. Jem and Pete grinned.

The Major and Dolly returned just before tea well pleased with themselves each other and their day together. Dolly went upstairs to take off her hat and tidy her hair before tea, where her daughter was waiting for her in their rooms. Caroline noticed her mother's sparkling eyes and happy smile, she had not seen her mother look quite like this since her father passed away several years ago and she was glad to see it.

"Well Mums had a good day?" She was smiling.

Dolly was busy powdering her nose before she brushed her hair.

"Well I must say I really did, a real gentleman, he took me to lunch in a lovely place too. Treated me like I was a queen."

Caroline grinned, "Mums! Good for you."

Dolly laughed happily "Well he did, and what is more wants me to go again with him and so I shall. He said my advice is really helpful. I must say the houses he is looking at are very nice too. One is beautiful."

Chapter 20

Caroline had changed into a pretty green floral tea gown, it showed off her deep red hair very well and she hoped Archie would notice she knew he was rather particular about the right clothes, She also wore her strappy leather green shoes and her fine pearl set.

"Come on I want my tea. I like the gallant Major but I really really like Archie."

"So do I dear, so do I, all of that."

The weather had turned suddenly colder and was raining heavily outside, it had turned dark early, the heavy curtains had been drawn to shut out the weather and tea was being served in the drawing room. A huge log fire burned in the grate, hot buttered muffins and cakes were handed round, a very British picture, Hiram and Charleen said "This was just what they had looked forward to." The last guest had arrived earlier Pete had been sent to the station to meet her. He had looked at her carefully she was a lovely dark haired girl, dressed in the very latest style, but what he really noticed was she looked vaguely familiar as he later told Chalfont. Jem helping with her luggage agreed with him.

"We seen her somewhere no mistake about that, just can't quite think where it was."

"She works for fashion papers."

"Well I don't look at them."

"A crook then do you think?"

"Possibly, unlikely though, will try to remember, seen her face somewhere though."

"Watch her very carefully that's what I say."

The women recognised the new guest immediately as Nancy Henderson, she wrote about the latest fashions. They noticed her very latest look dress and shoes with envy. Burgundy fine wool and beaded as were her matching leather high heeled shoes. She told them in a very smiling and friendly way she was back from New York where she had been living and working, she had been feeling homesick was tired and needed a little rest.

"Not that I don't love New York an exciting city, but I needed to come home for a while, family reasons and this looked like the ideal heavenly place while I find a flat in town before I begin my new job, and what do I get, a real proper, gorgeous English tea by a wonderful fire, this is absolute heaven, just what I have dreamed of and missed."

"We are glad to have you" said Shelly offering her a plate of buttery crumpets.

"I have to tell you please don't be alarmed if you see any stray policeman wandering about the place, they are very tame I assure you."

"Stray policemen?" asked Nancy looking faintly amused as she took a crumpet and bit into it..

"Yes they are investigating a murder that took place in the

coach house and are still sometimes looking about for clues I think, so every now and then the odd one pops out of the shrubs, it can make one jump." Shelly was trying to reassure her last guest.

"We found the poor old blighter in the boat house, seeing all life was extinct called the boys in blue do you see." Archie took over the tale.

"It was all rather horrid, we thought at first it was a tramp who had taken shelter and sadly died in there."

Nancy saw the quick glance between Archie and James and knew they had known it was not a natural death.

"How terrible for you" she said politely taking a sip of her tea. "I take it they know what happened and who it was, the victim I mean."

"Yes, don't want to go into detail and all that, but they took him away and identified him as a crook called Sam Jennings and think it was a case of thieves falling out, we think they were after the cars."

They didn't notice Nancy stiffen because at that moment Hiram snarled angrily "They are my darn cars now and they got me to deal with."

"OK Honey" said Charleen soothingly.

"With all the police making their presence known, your cars are pretty safe now, remember when the crime took place Lady Shelly was here alone, even Chalfont was in London" said James quietly.

Shelly shivered "It is not a nice feeling to think somebody was killed in my home."

Nancy asked "So they don't know who did it, or how was the poor man killed?"

Shelly shivered.

"With a heavy wrench, that's also the reason it took so long to identify him, horrid injuries, he was killed in the coach house and then his body hidden in the boat house. James found the weapon."

"I fell stupidly, and putting my hand out to save myself grabbed it sticking out of the wall." James was watching her as he told his tale.

"You found the weapon not the police" said Nancy quickly.

"Yes but you see" began James.

"And they were in trouble too about that" Archie laughed. Shelly looked at Charleen who was looking very pale suddenly.

"We seem to be talking about a very sad subject at the tea table."

"Sorry it is the journalist coming out in me" answered Nancy quickly. She smiled her apology.

The women all began to ask about the latest fashions, new hemlines and styles to come while the men went off to the billiards room, this was a deep intense feminine subject now that they were not included in.

Dolly didn't even bat an eye when she heard of the latest police visit, she had her Major to protect her now and she was sure he would do just that, Archie was following Caroline around all the time, she had been so right to bring them here, Archie was she was certain going to propose to her beloved daughter and he would be very suitable, not titled sadly but they were a perfect match and he would make her Caroline happy and Dolly wanted just that, she knew she herself was going to be.

Chapter 21

Dolly herself looked forward to spending more time with her Major or John as he asked her to call him, she smiled as she recalled that moment at lunchtime in the pretty little country pub. She was also thinking Croft Manor and how she would make it a wonderful home for them .She would be Mrs,Grimshaw-Peak who would have guessed,she was so glad she had come here,he was such a dear man and they would be very happy together.

After tea everyone was busy doing things of their own, although the weather had turned very cold and wet so nobody wanted to go outside. Nancy Henderson busy with the help of

Polly Shelley's maid unpacking and hanging up her beautiful and fashionable clothes. Polly would be reporting back to Shelly later with all the news about them. Shelly had planned to wear a stunning dark red silk gown that night, it was very simple and timeless, she looked wonderful in it, she had never worn it before and planned to make James really take notice, she would only wear some plain gold earrings and a pretty plain gold rope necklace, the dress would do the rest.

 The other ladies all planned their outfits carefully, they needed to be at their best with Nancy in their midst. They were very busy not knowing that Nancy had other things on her mind. She had come back to England to find her brother she had not seen him for years and now he was all the family she had left, him and her aunt.

 Hiram was talking to Dirk and telling him of his own plans. He planned to leave Charleen here, she was getting stronger and taking things very easy, she could rest and nap whenever she wanted and she loved being here. She didn't venture far outside and was being well cared for, if she needed anything she only had to ring the bell, yes this was the place for her for now. He however wanted to arrange to get his cars shipped home as soon as possible.

"I am not so sure they are safe here any more even if some louse can't steal them with all the cops around they could get damaged, once they are gone and safe at home I'll feel a darn sight better.

We can shoot some of the picture around here maybe, but we need to find some other places too, a quaint old town. Some famous British scenes. Ruth can stay and take care of Charleen, she needs some more time to recover, she was mighty sick there for a while, but I'd like you to come along with me, this picture is going to be the best we ever made. You will be carrying it all the way, give you a chance to show what you can really do. A part to get your teeth into. Maybe use a British actress as your leading lady some real class act I am thinking Sybil Dean, what do you say?"

Dirk was all for it and said so. He liked the idea of being involved in all the action, he didn't realize that Hiram wanted to keep him close and make sure he didn't start drinking heavily, it would also be a burden on Charleen and he wanted her to relax and get better.

They all met downstairs for drinks before dinner, all the ladies had taken special care with their look in honour of the famous fashion writer, she herself did too because she knew it would be expected of her, all the other women would be waiting to see what she wore, she was used to it, she wore a magnificent bronze coloured outfit that was the latest style, a slim fitting ankle length skirt and over the top a form fitting long brocade tunic of the same colour, it stopped just below her hips, and had black silk embroidery of an exotic design round the neck and down the long sleeves , the outfit was stunning and all the other women wanted it. She wore no jewels.

Shelly came down last for once she wanted to impress James in her red gown, although he stared at her for a moment and caught his breath he quickly looked away, he told himself she was not for him, he could never hope to win her. Shelly had her own ideas about that. She had noticed that look and smiled to herself.

Archie only had eyes for Caroline, he did not notice

anything else. He was deciding if he should tell her how he felt. Take his chances. They all had drinks and were talking when Chalfont announced dinner. When they were all sitting drinking coffee later, Hiram announced that he was arranging to get the cars shipped home, a team of drivers would be coming to take them away to put them on a ship and then taken to his home in California. Shelly felt a slight pang another link with her Father and Simon gone, she shook herself, this has to happen he had paid her what she had asked for and her home was saved. Archie getting up for another cup of coffee gave her arm a gentle squeeze in passing he knew just how she felt. James alone noticed this and wished he could comfort her, she looked so lovely in that red dress, like a queen.

    The next morning after breakfast Hiram and Dirk left, Hiram telling Charleen to take it easy and rest up. Shelly promised to make sure she did.

Chapter 22

James had a restless night his leg was hurting and he couldn't get comfortable also he could not get Shelly out of his mind, it had been a mistake coming here, he couldn't blame Archie only himself for being such a damn fool, falling in love with the only girl in the world for him, and the one he could never win, he had been in several battles, seen friends die and been wounded but none had hurt as badly as this. He was torn between packing up and returning home, he would do his best to forget her, or gritting his teeth and trying to help Archie protect her, surely once the cars were gone she would be safe but then Archie might have left with

Caroline as well, staying here with her alone would be frowned on, and what could he a damn invalid do to protect anyone, he had no right to be in her way, a nuisance was all he was. She would possibly get more guests. Then he remembered she had asked him to finish building Simon's car, how could he have forgotten? He could at least do that for her, a small comfort he could offer her, make himself useful in this way, he could not and would not let her down. He tossed and turned and tried to find a way to get comfortable enough to sleep, finally in the early hours of the morning he gave up and getting out of bed went over to put a small log on the glowing embers of the fire. Toby sat up in his basket and snuffled a damp nose into his hand as he sat in a chair by the fire, James poured himself a whiskey and sipped it by the light of the flickering flames, he sighed he thought it was still dark outside, too early to be up, he gently fondled Toby's head, the dog whined softly he was used to his master's nocturnal ways and seemed to understand why. Toby got up and went to the window, then he growled.

"What's up boy?" asked James wearily. He got up too and

went over to the window, he pulled back the curtains and looked out into the night, it was still dark but the sky had a few faint lighter streaks dawn was coming.

Something caught his eye a faint light coming from the coach house, surely Hiram wasn't out checking his cars this early. He suddenly felt angry instead, the bounder might be back, he was not letting him prowl about in Shelly's home again, he might damage Simon's car and he James had promised her he would build it. He grabbed his stick. Toby wagged his tail if they were going out for a walk he was happy.

"Sorry old boy not this time, I need to be quiet, back in your basket, good boy stay." Toby whined but did as he was told. James put his gun in his pocket and silently slipped out of the room. James crept downstairs, he thought about calling for Archie but decided it would take too much time, he'd need to wake him up first, he stopped and listened but there wasn't a sound, he continued on, he found the side door unlocked to his surprise, then he went out . He made his way round the house keeping close to the walls, dawn was coming so he stayed in the darkest places. It was very cold in the early hours and he was glad of his heavy coat and hat, a scarf muffled up round his face. He had reached the coach house the doors were ajar, he could hear two voices they seemed to be angry and he thought one was a woman, he crept up and peered in through the opening. He could just make out two figures in the gloom there was a faint light on the coming from the floor enough for him to see neither of the figures were looking in his direction, one voice was sneering. James silently slipped inside and flattened himself against the wall to listen. He wanted to get closer but didn't want to miss what they were saying, He heard the woman say something angrily then came a scuffle and the lights went out with a clatter just as the same time a shot rang out. Silence, not a sound. A few moments later James felt a sharp pain and slumped to the cold floor.

    Jem and Pete had heard a sound earlier and had come out to investigate, but they had heard it the other side of the house and were investigating there, then they heard the shot and came running towards it, they went into the coach house and fell over James's prone form just inside the door.

They cursed. Inside the house, lights were coming on and soon out came Chalfont, followed by the Major then Archie, they soon arrived, Archie was shocked to see his friend with Chalfont leaning over him. Chalfont spoke to the Major saying " He is alive sir."

"Jem, Pete carry him carefully back to the house" answered the Major.

"Now look here" began Archie angrily.

"All in good time dear fellow but we need to see to him first do you see."

"I shall call Dr Medway sir, said Chalfont and went on ahead. Shelly was just coming out of the front door tying up the belt of her dressing gown.

"What has happened? Did I hear a shot?" Then she saw Jem and Pete carrying James's still body between them Gripping her hands together she let out a long moan of horror.
Chalfont called "He has sustained a bump on the head My Lady, he is alive and I will call Dr Medway immediately" but Shelly was already running towards the rest of the group and James.

"Is he?" she asked plaintively. The Major took her arm and tucked it into his.

"He must have fallen and bumped his head, but he will do, your good Chalfont is calling the quack right away, this brave young fellow will be right as rain later, but I dare say will have a nasty headache."

She fought back her tears.

Archie was angry a shot had been fired,. What had happened did James fire at someone?

Of course that must have been it, but why the devil had he come out in the middle of the night and why hadn't he called for him, Archie also felt guilty this was all his fault he had brought his friend James here telling him it would be good for him and peaceful but fun, now he had been injured because of it, and who did this bally Major think he was, he was going to wait until James had seen the quack and then demand some answers, this was all a bit too much.

James still out cold was carried carefully upstairs and was slowly lain down on his bed, the Major gently removed his overcoat but still James made no sound. His head was bleeding.

Pete had carried his hat. Chalfont came in carrying a bowl of warm water and a clean cloth, Shelly took it from him and bathed James's head, she gave a little stifled sob when she saw the bruise.

"Dr Medway is on his way My Lady."

The Major was whispering to Jem and Pete, they left the room. Archie scowled at him.

"What the devil is this all about?" Archie asked angrily. The Major shook his head and pointedly looked at Shelly.

James looked so pale and still, she was so afraid, and then she dropped the bowl on the floor sobbing, lay her head on his chest, she seemed to have forgotten they were there or didn't care and to Archie's astonishment was between sobs saying "Oh James my dearest James! Please come back to me, don't go, don't leave me, I simply cannot bear to lose you too, there is nothing on earth worth that. Please be well again."

As they all watched a hand was shakily lifted and began to softly caress her hair, James eyes fluttered open. Shelly turned and kissed him. The Major beamed at the astonished Archie and patted him on the back.

Chalfont left the room and was soon back with some tea helped by a scared looking young maidservant.

"The other ladies of the house are still asleep, it is still early they are not aware of anything that has happened."

"Then let's have some restorative tea, so we can keep it that way, no need to disturb or alarm them, at all."

"Very good sir."

"Now look here what is the meaning of this?" asked Archie in a quiet menacing voice.

Shelly was holding a cup for James and the two of them glanced round, James winced with the effort of moving his head and Shelly chided him. She put more pillows behind him and he lay back with a sigh.

"It was worth it for this my love" he said taking her hand.

Chalfont coughed and said "I believe I heard the doctor" and with that he left to let him in.

The Major spoke quietly "James here couldn't sleep and went for a stroll, he slipped and bumped his head. Trust me I will explain later."

"Why the dickens should we say that? He was attacked, and why haven't the police been called, I should like to know, what the devil is going on here? We all heard that gunshot, was that you old boy?"

James said "No, I heard an argument the some sort of scuffle, then a shot as the light went out, after that somebody gave out a sort of sigh and before I could find out anything I got biffed from the side."

Shelly held his hand looking at him with wide frightened eyes.

"This can't be allowed to go on, I am calling the police" snapped Archie.

"No police, trust me on this dear chap, we can handle this best ourselves, let me explain first after the doctor has been, and then if you are still of a mind to you can call them later, let's get this brave young man fixed up first to put our girl's mind at rest, I can hear him coming up the stairs now. Remember fell, bumped head, it will be better that way I tell you."

Dr Medway came in and saw them "I believe I have one patient who has had a wee accident" he said scooting them out with his hands, they left, Shelly reluctantly.

Chalfont asked behind them "Shall I serve an early breakfast for you My Lady? Mrs Barclay is in the kitchen and ready to start it, I took the liberty to say Mr Lakeland had taken a tumble and would require his in his rooms."

"If I may make a suggestion, we could have a breakfast up here with James in his sitting room, I know you all need answers and so does he, we keep him company and I will tell you a story or as much as I know so far" said the Major.

"I bet you will tell us a story" muttered Archie under his breath.

"Yes please serve breakfast in James's sitting room, he can have his in bed and with the door open hear us."

"Very good My Lady. I shall do so as soon as Dr Medway has finished seeing him."

"Excellent I am famished" answered the Major. Archie glared at him.

Dr Medway opened the door and Shelly went forward, "Your young man says he fell and bumped his head," he said shaking his head. "He will do, but he needs rest and to stay in bed quietly not that I think he will listen to me, but maybe to you, I have left him some medicine, foul tasting stuff as all good medicines should be , make him take it, it will ease that nasty headache he has, he will be getting a bigger bump come up yet, no excitement, he'll be drowsy so don't let him go wandering about, I have given him one dose, take good care of him" he said with another shake of his head. "Fell over indeed." they heard him mutter as he went downstairs.

    Soon Chalfont was back with two housemaids, tables were arranged, the fires made up, James was sitting back now in some very natty silk pyjamas against his pillows, he had a light bandage around his head Treach smoothed the covers before he left.

Shelly bent and kissed his cheek carefully. Breakfast was served, James was given his on a tray,

"As soon as breakfast is over I would like you here too Chalfont, this is as much your story as anybodies, and also you can fill in any details that I might not be aware of" said the Major. "But for now I am tucking into this delicious food, the story is a long one and we need to eat up first."

Archie looked at Chalfont with a puzzled look on his face this was getting curiouser and curiouser.

"Very good sir."

A short time later Chalfont was back and said "Excuse me sir there has been an occurrence, a body has been found in the coach house .

"What! Exclaimed Archie and Shelly together.

"Ah so we were right" said the Major. "Was it who we suspected?"

"Yes sir, a Mr. Coulter, he had been shot through the head."

"That does it, we have to call the rozzers now, even if it was that rotten blighter, can't have bodies appearing all over the place dash it, we will be finding corpses on the doorstep next" said Archie hotly.

" As you so rightly said that rotten blighter and he was far more rotten than you know, please allow me to tell you why and then you can decide if you still want to call the rozzers as you put it. There is no more danger now I assure you, and this story will explain everything and is of course for your ears only and not for anyone else. You will understand why."

Archie snorted.

Chapter 23

After the breakfast things were cleared away they all took chairs into James's bedroom, he was now laying back against his pillows still looking very pale but happy with a lock of blonde hair falling over his bandage, Shelly loved him he knew, and that was all he could care about, he was feeling very tired though. Chalfont came in with a tray of coffee and told them the other ladies were still asleep as it was still early, he also gave the Major a little nod before standing behind Shelly.

The Major said "Thankyou, good, now this story began a long time ago before you were born but you need to hear all of it. I know two of you young rascals cast me as the villain of the piece much to my great amusement but then why shouldn't you have, you after all you have never met me before." He laughed and raised a hand before they could answer and then with a twinkle in his eye told them.

"You only had to ask Chalfont he knows who I am, we met several times, our paths crossed here and in India. They were all silent and listening intently. "As I said it all began a long time ago, Lord Ralf, Robert Stewart, a young Indian Prince who shall remain nameless for private reasons and I were all the best of chums at school and then university, we we up to all kinds of tricks and never far apart." He stopped with a smile of pleasant memories and took a sip of his coffee.

"Ah yes, then towards the end of our term we were invited by Rob's father the old laird to visit his home a castle, it was on a remote island off the Scottish Highlands. Raj, yes let's call him Raj we all did, was very excited at the thought of visiting a Scottish castle, one where his chum grew up, we had already been invited to visit India someday. So we packed up our traps and caught the train to bonny Scotland, we were in the very best of spirits planning to stay over Christmas and see in the New Year too.

"Four of the best of chums nothing would ever come between our friendship. Well I won't give you all the details you can use your own imagination, young lads swearing oaths to fight off anything together. The important bit is the first night after we arrived Rob introduced us to his father the Laird and his sister the Lady Elspeth, and she was a real beauty I can tell you, one of the most beautiful girls I have ever seen, long curly hair the colour of wine, it was such a deep dark red and her eyes were as green as emeralds, she truly was something special, well of course we all fell a little bit in love with such a beauty, all except poor Raj who fell like a ton of coals deeply and madly in love." He looked round at all of them.

"We didn't of course realize that at first, he was always falling for some pretty girl or other, but this was the real thing. Near the end of the visit Raj had declared himself, and Elspeth who had fallen in love with the handsome young Indian prince accepted, of course he should have asked the laird for permission to court her first but he had fallen in love and wanted to know how she felt first, he was afraid she would reject him and he would have kept the whole thing to himself so we didn't rag him unfeeling young bounders as we were. So Raj first told Rob and asked how to go about asking the laird for her hand. Well as you can imagine all hell broke loose, Rob challenging Raj to a duel for seducing his sister, insulting his family and him by slyly using his friendship and invitation to his home abusing their hospitality to mess about with his sister behind their backs and so on. There was a mighty and terrible row, we all heard it and came running to see what was happening including the laird who bellowed to be told what was the meaning of all this rumpus? Elspeth came in and began to cry, She said she loved Raj and wanted to be his wife.

  Rob turned on her and called her a vile name, Raj punched him. She was led away sobbing by an aunt and we saw her no more. The laird by then was furious and demanded quite rightly answers for this behaviour and why his innocent beloved daughter had been called the name by her brother.

  "What madness is this?" he roared

Rob of course told him. The laird was outraged, how dare this brown skinned heathen foreigner dare to presume he could court his precious girl, such a thing could never be allowed, and to do so behind his back made it even worse, disgraceful behaviour, the upshot was Raj, Ralf and I were told to sling our collective hooks, we were kicked out immediately and we caught a train back to London after a freezing night spent on a railway station. Rob did come back to university but refused to speak to us, Ralf and I tried, we had been such friends after all but he would have none of it and Raj was just as stubborn, he said they had done nothing wrong, and vowed to wed the fair Elspeth somehow and he was also sad and worried about her. Rob became friends with some others including the cad Coulter they were all much younger than us. A couple of months later Raj was called home to India his father was seriously ill. To cut a long story shorter Ralf and I were recruited to err serve our country, I can say no more about the things we did except to tell you Ralf found and recruited our good Chalfont here and much later young Jem and Pete who are even now working in our best interests, you can trust Chalfont completely, your father did my dear."

"Indeed his lordship asked me to keep Lady Shelly safe and not leave her if anything should happen to him" answered Chalfont. Shelly smiled at him her eyes shining with tears Daddy had always made sure she was well cared for. She missed him and Simon so much She would have been lost without Chalfont.

"I have always trusted and relied on my dear Chalfont.."

"Thank you My Lady."

"Please continue Major."

"Well let me see where was I? Ah yes Ralf and I were sent over to visit Raj, his father had died and he was the new Maharaja and an important friend of this country. As we were known to be his friends it was thought we would be the best for the job to seal the bond between our countries it was a pleasure of course. Ralf took Chalfont and we were instructed to do all in our power to show our countries willingness to offer any assistance to the new Maharaja that he may need, at the time we found this most amusing. Well we found Raj now every inch the king he was born to be but not a happy one, he lacked one thing, he was pleased to see us we were the ones he could tell that what he wanted most of all was his Elspeth at his side as his queen. So I stayed on in India a place I loved, to work for Raj and also England. Ralf and Chalfont returned home with some idea that now Raj was a powerful ruler the laird may see things differently. Ralf and I were not so sure but Ralf said he would try. Chalfont can tell the next bit, you can much better than me after all you were there."

"With your permission My Lady?"

"Oh yes please tell us, this is fascinating."

"His Lordship and I returned home and secretly went up to Scotland, His Lordship hired a small cottage and a boat, his plan was to stay hidden and try and find out what was going on, after all what if Elspeth had wed? We did not want to see Rob or Coulter if he were there, his Lordship really detested the latter."

Shelly and Archie gasped this was all news to them.

"All in good time my dears" said the Major.

"Yes of course" said Shelly quietly "Please continue Chalfont."

"Very good My Lady, we decided to row over to the island

where the castle was, it was a fine Spring morning and we hoped to find a young maidservant and ask her about Lady Elspeth, young women would always be willing to talk to his Lordship" he chuckled.

    Shelly smiled at this she knew beloved father all too well

    "We were in luck, the first thing we saw was a young woman walking across the heather alone, she had her head bowed and a shawl wrapped around her head and shoulders when suddenly a gust of wind caught at it and blew it back to release a cloud of long red curls, it was Lady Elspeth herself and she was weeping bitterly. Lord Ralf ever a gentleman stepped out from the trees we were hiding in, he could never bear to see a lady weep, and so at first with a squeak of fright and then a sob of joy when she recognised him she rushed forward and threw herself into his Lordship's arms. She thought Raj was with us just for a moment but then told us she guessed he had forgotten all about her now just as Rob had been taunting her. We assured her that was not the case he loved her still as we went back into the trees, " For I dare not be seen with you, Rob is not the brother I used to know and love he has become somebody I do not know any more, him and that awful Coulter. So now I am given a choice by my father marry a man who is a friend of his and I can't abide or stay locked away here and not go anywhere, never to meet any visitors. I did nothing wrong I fell in love with my beautiful Raj and I will always be in love with him. I am afraid Rob will want me to marry that sly Coulter when my father dies.

There have been times when I think of jumping from one of the towers, it seems my only way out. I will never wed Dougal. I am so unhappy now but I am so happy to see you, how did you get to the island? If that sly sneaky Coulter who follows me around sees you he will sure to go running to my father."

"Do you really want to go to Raj and a strange country so very different from your own, leave every thing you have behind? You will never be able to return you know" said his Lordship. "We have a boat that we came here in."

"Where is the boat moored? I will leave it all behind gladly to be with my one true love. Please take me with you now there is very little time before they come looking for me and then it will be too late this is my only chance."

The listeners were all agog and silent..

"And that was that, she ran with us as fleet as a deer and jumped into the boat, hid herself while we had grabbed our few belongings from the tiny cottage in the cove where the boat was tied up. Lady Elspeth was very anxious to go at once but we explained we could not leave anything to show who had been there. I remember how they both were laughing, when we were rowing away. There was now turning back now. We had got away and soon found a ship bound for India."

Shelly her eyes sparkling clapped her hands. "Oh what a wonderful story how brave you and Daddy were how gallant."

The Major once again took over the story "Raj was so happy and delighted he wanted to reward Ralf who had freed and given him his greatest treasure his beloved princess. but Ralf refused to take anything of course. Elspeth and Raj got married a huge affair and they are very happy, she gave him three fine sons, they all four adore her. Of course your father had done a great service to England creating an unbreakable bond between the countries but the reason was played down as much as possible over here but not by the new Maharaja. Ralf quietly returned home where shortly after he met and fell madly in love with your beautiful mother, you are very like her my dear. You know some of the rest how they were happily married and so on, but not the bits where your father still did great services to our country and I cannot of course tell you about them. Later Ralf had to return to India we shall not say why but he stayed with Raj and Elspeth she was very very fond of your father and so was Raj. I was happy to see Ralf and we yarned for hours, he told me one day when I retired and returned home to England to come and live nearby so we could live out our last and peaceful years together. I agreed to this fine idea.

  Your mother had sadly died and he missed her very much." Shelly wiped her eyes and James held her hand he was trying hard to stay awake. Even the Major and Archie's eyes were moist, Chalfont kept his head bowed down.

  "Well at last it was time for them to return home, Raj and Elspeth were determined to show their gratitude for all Ralf and

Chalfont too had done for them, their story would have been so different and not the happy bliss they had now, and so with a little help from me one of your Father's trunks got damaged and so I gave him an old one of mine, we laughed at how battered it looked but believe me it was very strong and well made, it also had a false bottom. So Raj gave me some gold and also uncut precious stones to insert, I told Chalfont after it had been loaded on board the ship bound for England, there were some for him too in a separate bag hidden with them. He had played his part. He promised to give them to Ralf when they were safely home in Rosewood Hall. I understand they are still remain hidden "

All doubts Archie had about the Major had vanished.

"Good show sir, what a fine tale, so they really do exist ?"

"They do indeed my sir, when we arrived home his Lordship was very amused when I gave them to him, he told me that he would put them away somewhere safe here for his children to find later as he had no need for them himself. He hadn't wanted to be rewarded for helping his friends to find happiness. He insisted I took mine, then I know he hid them here somewhere, but where I do not know, I believe he kept moving them finding different places. I did search many times for Lady Shelly when she needed them, I had no luck finding them but he definitely did not take them anywhere else I am certain of that" said Chalfont.

"Golly how exciting and also annoying, Thank you for trying Chalfont, I have searched a few times myself. Simon told me about them years ago. We must combine efforts next time."

"May I suggest when the other guests have gone My Lady, I searched their rooms thoroughly before they arrived so there is no danger of one of them finding them."

"Excellent idea, now about that, I have retired now and came back to England, I have been staying with an elderly aunt not far away from here after Chalfont had sent me a message to tell me my dear friend and his son had been killed and he did not believe it was an accident. I came home to investigate, also I wanted to keep my dear friend's daughter safe with our trusty Chalfont's help."

"But you let her get engaged to that bounder Coulter!" said Archie.

James exclaimed "What."

"It was nothing dearest ,I don't even know why I agreed to it, I didn't even like him, but he said he was a friend of my fathers. I was so unhappy and missed daddy so much, Coulter was so much older and I thought he could take on all the worry like daddy had done, I felt nothing just numb, he asked me to marry him, he didn't even try to kiss me thank goodness, and then after giving me a ring that I didn't wear, he immediately went away and didn't bother me or try to visit I am very glad to say and I forgot all about him. I would not have married him really. Everything seemed grey and unreal somehow, I didn't want any visitors. Then when I thought about it I broke the engagement off it was never announced anyway as I was in mourning."

"She was perfectly safe, I admit it was a shock but he was too cunning to visit her or harm her, not with our good friend Chalfont as her guardian angel, and then Jem and Pete. Oh yes we had our eye on Coulter for a long time as did your Father."

"A wedding would never have taken place" said Chalfont in a steely cold voice.

"Indeed not" said the Major.

Archie looked shocked then looked over and saw the grin on James's face so he returned it.

"Coulter was a thoroughly rotten egg through and through he could turn on the charm when it suited his purpose of course but don't doubt it for a moment he was really evil. We guessed he was spying too and must have somehow got wind of the jewels perhaps Simon told a friend and Coulter found out, he liked to throw parties get young men drunk and find out secrets that way. He told Rob we know that Ralf had sold Elspeth for gold, he did it just to cause trouble but he himself was after the jewels of course."

"Nothing could have been further from the truth My Lady, your father refused a reward, he just helped two friends " said Chalfont quickly.

"I know Chalfont and I am glad he had you with him. Coulter was a hateful beast, I didn't know how much but I never would have married him. I came to my senses, and thank you for taking such good care of me."

"It has always been my pleasure to do so My Lady."

"I second that well done Chalfont" said a sleepy voice from

the bed.

"After Chalfont informed me what had occurred I came home this time for good as I said and was determined to find out the truth as well as to meet and protect Lady Shelly. I really have retired but can still pull strings, of course I had things to deal with in London first we had to find a way to deal with Coulter once and for all, I knew Lady Shelly was in good hands, also she not going out anywhere. I had been too late to my regret to be here with my old friend but I am really looking for a house and think I have found one that Dolly and I can be happy in, oh yes she has agreed to marry me."

The others were all delighted to hear this and said so.

"And young man, she will be very happy to have you as a son- in- law as will I. She thinks you may be toying with her dear daughter as she comes from humble beginnings but I reassured her telling her I did not believe that for a moment" the Major said with a twinkle in his blue eyes.

Archie hadn't seen it and so at first blustered very red in the face

"No No that is not the case at all! The fact of the matter is Caroline is so wealthy, I am not a pauper don't you know but can't match her, not a fortune hunter johnny you see. Didn't think my proposal would be welcomed by her mother " He then looked at the Major and saw his smile.

"Nonsense my dear boy, Dolly wants her daughter to be happy and Caroline has assured her you are it, they are both waiting for you to ask, and if I were you and it's what you want to do, future happiness don't you see, don't let some fortune hunter rotter get near her."

Archie didn't know when he had liked the Major more, he was an excellent man how foolish he had been to doubt him.

"I will certainly do so at the first possible chance."

" That's the spirit. Now on to other things before the other ladies are up. This is why I don't think we should call the police, firstly it will alarm the other ladies, the police will be all over the place looking for clues and motives We know what they were and I will prove them later, the story can come to an end with no more threats to Lady Shelly's safety. If you wish to call the police consider this, Hiram won't be able to take his cars for sometime yet again and he is away making arrangements to do so. Lady Shelly won't get her home back for sometime and I am sure as charming as we all are she wants to get on and marry that young man in the bed over there and also live in peace. She has the money from Hiram for the cars and doesn't need to keep this paying guest lark all the time, also Hiram has paid for his cars and it's only fair that he can take them away or he may get fed up lose interest and want his money back."

"Oh no no no!" gasped Shelly "I don' t want that to go through all that again and perhaps see the collection broken up."

"Precisely!" said the Major.

"Although I agree with all this, two murders have been committed here and how do you know that will be the last, there is a murderer on the loose and there is also the matter of a body out there won't it be noticed soon? Well when Hiram gets back for sure. Are you saying you know who the murderer is?" asked Archie.

"Certainly! Coulter murdered the first man and I am

dealing with the second, before you say any more and your respect for the law does you credit, we would be placing our local rozzers in an awkward position. I must explain that this is a case of national security and I am still part of that, also if the police are called in we can't tell the whole story, think of the scandal, it could cause a serious international problem, just think of how the gutter press will love it. We could not stop it or hush it up and news of hidden jewels getting out not only the press will be here in a flash with journalists popping out of bushes waving note books at you every time you stick your nose out of doors, the jewel thieves will be prowling about at night trying to get in and search the house, even possibly bumping each other off to cut the competition. you won't be able to call the place your own. Think how they would write a tale of a British lord kidnapping a beautiful young titled lady for an Indian prince, everyone would be reading all the details some heavily embroidered over the breakfast table. That is what would happen ."

"No! No! No! said Shelly firmly. "Absolutely not, enough is enough, I will not let that filthy beast Coulter do any more to harm my family and that is that. I am going to marry my darling James as soon as possible, he came here for peace and quiet and that is what he is going to get. Tell us what to do, we can easily bury Coulter in the woods and none will be the wiser, I will do it myself if that is what it takes. The only person who will know is his killer and I am sure he won't mind."

James chuckled "You won't have to do it alone."
Archie who knew her so well said calmly and agreed in principal "Have you forgotten he bashed James on the bonce, how do you know he isn't still lurking around, and who will be his next victim?"

The Major spoke again "I know that won't happen, I came here as I said before to find out the truth and make the man pay for the murder of my dearest and oldest friend and his son." He turned and looked straight at Shelly now.

"This will be painful for you my dear but they were murdered by Coulter. He was a spy selling secrets, a traitor working against our country as well as a ruthless killer, we had been after him for years but he was a sly and cunning evil bounder and we could find no proof, I believe your father was finally onto him with something that could bring him down and so Coulter killed them. I am so very sorry I wasn't here to prevent it."

Shelly was weeping softly and James held her gently in his arms.

Archie snarled " The filthy snake. Where are the spades? We will dig later when it's dark."

"It will be taken care of and no questions asked, no traces left not a one." The Major gave Chalfont a little nod and Chalfont silently left the room. "So now to finish this part of the story before moving on to better and happier times."

Chapter 24

"This next bit is going to be a bit tricky, you need to hear it too, you are now of course sworn to keep all of this, every word secret. Listen but please keep quiet, leave it all to me, we will come about. Are you willing to do so?" They all agreed wondering what would happen next. Shelly had dried her tears or rather James had, he was still holding her and trying to stay awake determined to finish hearing the end of the story..

"I never believed my father had been drinking and driven the car he would never ever had done that. I am glad to have been told the truth at last and glad Coulter is dead, whoever killed him deserves a medal."

"That may happen strangely enough" said the Major quietly.

Just then Chalfont came back in holding the door open wide for Nancy Henderson who was followed closely by Jem and Pete. She had a defiant and sullen look on her face. She was very angry and scowled at Jem.

"What's the meaning of this? These two thugs have kept me prisoner in my room. I need to get back to London urgently, a new job, I left a note for you Lady Shelly because it's so early and I will be back in a few days. When I tried to leave they took my bag and they grabbed me and kept me locked in my room, it's outrageous. I demand to be able to leave. Since when did a paying guest become a prisoner? " she snarled.

The Major raised his eyebrows and stared at her then he answered, "When they commit two murders. Tell me why you did it, the truth now Nancy Henderson or should I say Nancy Jennings?"

Everyone in the room gasped.

Nancy glared at him " If you know so much you know that is not true. I did not commit two murders. Very well you seem to know some of it but not all, I did not kill my brother, and how did you know he was?"

"It is my business to know these things, Jem and Pete said you looked familiar, they knew your brother quite well, the rest was easy, may I suggest you tell me the whole story, it will make it easier for yourself, I was not a friend of Coulter who you most definitely did kill".

Nobody else spoke they all waited for her to answer. Chalfont pulled out a chair for her and she sat down, then Nancy shrugged and lifted her head proudly.

"Our father was a real rotter he treated my mother dreadfully he was very handy with his fists when he had been drinking so one day she left taking me, Sam wanted to say with dad.

Mum got a job as a maid and I was allowed to stay with her, as a companion for the little daughter of the house, she was very frail we got on well and became friends. The nursery maid left and mum got her job it was all so good. The family moved to America and asked mum to go too to look after the little girl on the ship, she jumped at the chance. A new start. I went to school and then later college over there and loved it all. My father died in a drunken brawl, mum's sister wrote and told her, later mum met and married an American, they were very happy, he was a wonderful husband and I had a real dad who treated me like his own, put me through college, I did well and got my job. My mum and dad got sick that flu and died within days of each other." She stopped and shook her head, blinked fiercely then continued, "It happened and I was heartbroken. I kept working hard and got promoted, I loved my job, I was offered an assignment in London so I came over, I am sorry I ever did. I had an idea of finding and visiting what was left of my family, I had a vague sort of memory of an older brother." She stopped and took a deep breath, nobody spoke they all listened.

"May I have a glass of water? I had no breakfast and I feel a little faint." She was given one and fresh coffee was brought in. Some toast for her too.

"Thank you, I had only a vague idea where my aunt lived, so after I had finished the job I decided to look her up before returning to New York. I found her, she was delighted to see me, she told me many stories about my mum growing up, they had loved each other.

Dad was another story, she did not think he was any loss to the world, she told me he was a petty crook and had brought Sam up to be the same, she saw Sam from time to time he was always about to make a fortune somehow. She hadn't asked him any questions just gave him a hot meal. Lovely story isn't it!"

She did not expect or wait for an answer. "My aunt Joan told me she had seen Sam a few weeks ago and he was full of a new job working for some big toff he said, he was going to be rich, made for life, he would see she was given some money too to keep her in her old age. She had heard it all before many times. She said Sam was very excited, and would be out of town for a while. To cut a long story shorter I traced him to a cottage in a village a few miles from here where he was staying with Coulter, I had no idea who he was or what they were up to then. I had seen

Lady Shelly's advertisement and came here I wanted to meet my brother on my own terms, my aunt had made me want to, I had hoped I could possibly help him the way my American dad had helped me, I wanted to get to know him and offer him a chance to come back to New York with me, give him a fresh chance." She dashed a defiant tear from her eyes and the Major gave her his hanky, she blew her nose.

"I got such a shock when I heard he had been murdered here, I was determined to find out who did it, who took away the chance I had of meeting my big brother and his chance of a new start. Then in the middle of that night I heard a noise, I took my gun of course, I always travel with it and this time knowing a killer was on the loose here I was taking no chances if I needed to defend myself. I crept quietly into the coach house and saw a figure searching for something it seemed, he had put a lantern down and was looking away from me so I got close to him before he realised I was there. Then he turned and saw me. At first he was angry but I acted all chummy I wanted to find out who he was. I acted the dumb American broad, he had no idea and thought to try and use me for access to the house. That suited me just fine so I played along, he asked me a lot of questions and they were nearly all about Lady Shelly, he knew she had guests but not who, he very foolishly didn't ask who I was, he was so very anxious to know about Lady Shelly so I thought I could use that and get him mad then he would give more away, I wanted to be certain it was he who had murdered Sam, I kept my gun hidden behind my back, my plan was to get him to let enough slip to be sure, then I would hold the gun on him, march him over to the house and get Chalfont to call the police, how was I to know you were already here. So I giggled and told him how cute it was that Lady Shelly had a beau in the house and it sure looked like the real thing. He went pop eyed, and cursed, he said furiously he had had a guy working to him who turned out to be useless and also seemed to be planning on double crossing him so he had got rid of him. He laughed and said the idiot wouldn't ever double cross him again he had made sure of that." She paused for breath.

"He was so furious he blurted it all out saying the fool hadn't told him what was happening in the house and he was glad he was dead, not thinking I went cold and asked if he had killed the guy, he snarled realizing he had said too much and told me I had better keep my mouth shut, instead I told him who I was. I knew I was in danger. His face went dark with rage and fear as he saw the gun in my hand pointed at him, he kicked the lamp over and the place went pitch black, he lunged at me I tried to dodge but there wasn't any room I knew he would kill me if he could so I fired. I turned to run and heard a sound, someone else was there, one of his men, so I tried to creep out of there quietly holding my breath but realized the other guy was right in my way, I hit out with the gun and ran out into the darkness, I could hear other folks coming and I wanted to get away. I hoped nobody would see me, I had never met this Coulter guy before and thought nobody would link me to this mess."

"She is telling the truth of what happened with Coulter in the coach house at least" said a very drowsy voice from the bed.

Nancy looked startled as she looked over at James, her face suddenly dismayed.

"Say just what is going on and are you the good guys or the

bad guys? What have I walked into? Did you? Were you the other guy in the coach house? Sure I killed Coulter I admit it, it was me or him and I wasn't about to let him kill me. I told you all I know so will somebody please explain to me what is happening here?"

"Well young lady I believe your story and we are very much the good guys. I had been after Coulter for years but the slippery blighter always hid his tracks well. He was a bounder of the worst kind and a traitor to this country as well as a murderer."

"So I did you guys a good turn by accident, and by the way talking of that?"

"I was in the coach house because I heard a noise, didn't know what was up, sorry I put the wind up you" said James softly

"Oh no it is me that is so so sorry, I didn't know it was you, after Coulter attacked me I just lashed out in panic. I thought it was another of his men. I was scared and wanted out, I am so very sorry I hurt you."

James grinned sheepishly at her "As a matter of fact you did me a good turn too, it turned out rather well for me, worth getting bashed for, you could say." She saw Shelly holding his hand and nodded.

"So she killed that snake Coulter? He killed her brother. But what do we do now?" asked Archie in a dazed voice. .

"Remember Coulter murdered my Father and Simon too, she did a good thing as far as I'm concerned, rid the world of an evil louse I am even willing to forgive her for hurting my James now I know he will be better soon."

James raised her hand and kissed it,

" That's my fierce girl and I agree, we must do all we can to help her" he said before the sedative finally took hold and he fell asleep. Just before he slipped into a deep and peaceful sleep he sighed one cryptic word "Geese."

They all after giving James a puzzled look, turned to face the Major.

Chalfont made a queer snorting sort of cough as Lady Shelly asked "How do we get rid of the body?.

The Major said "Leave it all to me, now we must all agree quickly to secrecy and swear not to reveal what has happened, it fact it never did. This is a situation kept hidden for the sake of national security and you must all swear to it before the other ladies get up and that will be soon now, do you all agree?"

They all said "Agreed" together. Nancy gave a huge sigh of relief.

"Now Miss Henderson you showed some very useful traits tracking and finding your brother, sadly too late to save him but that was not your fault, great courage facing Coulter alone and you have shown other qualities, I can use a resourceful young woman like you, there is a job working for our country if you want it."

"Oh yes yes, I would like that very much. Just tell me what you want me to do" she said eyes brilliant with excitement.

"Good it would be a great waste to put a resourceful girl like you in prison or worse when you could be serving your old country."

"I will gladly do it, sounds like my life just got a whole lot better and more interesting."

"That settles that then, you are serving this great country as an agent, you tracked and executed a dangerous spy and enemy of the crown and England. That was your first job and no need to involve anybody else, The body will disappear without a trace later and the other ladies need not be bothered with such things. Hiram can take his cars. This is the best outcome I will deal with everything. I suggest we leave James with his dreams of geese in peace."

"No we mustn't upset the ladies not a good idea at all" agreed Archie.

Chapter 25

They all silently left the room Shelly hugged Nancy as they both shed tears. The evil Coulter had murdered both of their family members, Shelly thought Nancy was a brave woman and told her so.

The other women were all up dressed and breakfasted when they found them by this time having coffee in the morning room Shelly explained that James had taken Toby for an early walk and had slipped on the icy flagstones, to stem any awkward questions she followed this quickly with the news they were engaged, and were not making a formal announcement yet as his father was ill.

"Oh Honey congratulations, I could see the way that young man looked at you so sweetly I expect he was in a daydream and didn't watch his footing" said Charleen.

"Well done you two" said Caroline.

"Where is the dear boy?" asked Dolly.

"He is resting in bed on doctor's orders, in fact sleeping, Archie and our dear Major made sure he went to bed, he will be up and about in a day or two, possibly earlier if he has a say on the matter. The medicine has made him drowsy though."

The Major was having a quiet word in his own room with Chalfont, Pete and Jem, they told him now they know why she looked so familiar, she looked a lot like her brother. Nancy had left the room with them, to her surprise they all shook hands with her, then they explained she had their respect for killing the swine who murdered their Guv.

Meanwhile Archie took Caroline off to the conservatory, telling her softly he has something to say, she followed him out with a small half smile, Dolly and the Major exchanged meaningful looks watching them go. Chalfont told Charleen she is wanted on the telephone, she went off to answer with a smile having being given permission to tell Hiram about James and Shelly, The Major and Dolly retired to her sitting room to wait and see what news Caroline would bring.

Shelly went up to check on James, she saw he was asleep, a lock of thick blonde hair falling across his forehead , she looked lovingly over at him from the doorway, her future husband, she silently closed the door and turned to go to her own rooms. Shelly began playing with her cats by the fire feeling very happy when Chalfont appeared after knocking on her door "Excuse me My Lady, a large crate arrived at the station for Mr. Lakeland this morning, they telephoned earlier, you were rather busy and he had warned me he was expecting it so I took the liberty of getting old Tomkins to collect it and bring it up to the closed barn, it is a gift to you from Mr Lakeland's Mother."

"Goodness, I had better go and find out what it is, a large crate you say and it's in the closed barn."

"Yes My Lady and if I might make so bold you will need thick boots and warm clothes, it has started to snow, Pete is ready to accompany you and assist in opening the crate."

"Thank you Chalfont always so thoughtful what would I do without you."

"I would like to congratulate you on your happy news, I believe your Father would have approved of your choice."
She smiled "I too think he would have."

Shelly and Pete looked at the big wooden crate and then Pete opened it carefully at one end, then out came strutting and hissing eight white geese. Shelly laughed "So that is what he had meant."

"They do make fine watch dogs, and very fierce guards My Lady" said Pete with a grin, he left the crate open down one side and filled it with more hay as bedding. The geese began to explore the barn, Jem had appeared with food for them. Shelly laughing at her new fierce snow white guards went back to the house, the two men left the door open, the geese now had the run of the grounds, any new intruders had better beware.

Later James helped by Archie came down for dinner, he looked pale, but happy when he saw Shelly waiting for him. She told him she loved the geese. He laughed. Later over drinks Archie announced his engagement to Caroline, Dolly was full of plans for a huge wedding in London for them.

Dolly and her Major would be married first a small wedding with only close friends and family before they moved into their house it was the first one they had looked at and not to far from Rosewood Hall she announced.

James quietly asked Shelly where Nancy had got to and she told him Nancy had left quietly earlier just disappeared for the Major, no questions asked. The coach house had been cleaned up too nobody had seen a thing. Nancy and Shelly had said goodbye in Shelly's own rooms the two women hugged and wished each other well. Shelly told the others a story that Nancy had an exciting new job offer and had said to say goodbye as she had to leave suddenly, There were a few sad remarks but everyone was full of their own news.

After dinner they all sat by a big log fire in the drawing room, Chalfont busy serving coffee and brandies. Charleen told them Hiram would be back as soon as the roads were clear enough,

Shelly glanced over at the Major, "Call me Uncle John as Simon did" and he gave her a little nod, it all all been taken care of. Even though it was snowing. Shelly sighed and smiled at him.

    A couple of days later Hiram and Dirk returned with a crew of men who would drive away the cars, he congratulated all of them, had no idea what had really been happening here , if only he had, what a film he could have made, but he was happy full of taking his wonderful car collection and his new film, he had found the perfect locations and so he and Charleen said fond farewells and drove away the next morning. He had hired a house there for them.

Chapter 26

James and Shelly got married quietly in the little village church, James's father was still too ill to travel and so only his brother and sister came from his family, they loved Shelly at once. Shelly wore a white velvet and lace gown and a silk lined hooded cloak, it had been her mothers, with it she wore white boots, James looked at her adoringly as she came into the church on Uncle John's arm, she was his beautiful bride and James was so happy, he had not believed he could win her heart.

The whole village turned out to watch and many a tear was shed as she stopped after the ceremony to place her bouquet on her father's and brother's grave. A huge wedding feast was set up for the people in the village hall, bonfires burning brightly outside to light up the cold day. James and Shelly called in and had a toast drank to them before the happy pair went back home, the village party went happily on well into the night.

James and Shelly had the wedding they wanted and feasted with their own family and friends. The Major, Uncle John had given her away and Archie had been best man, Caroline and James's sister Sarah had been her bridesmaids, wearing cherry red gowns. Dolly was matron of honour to her great pleasure.. All the staff were included of course, Shelly had her new footmen Jem and Pete serving too, she suspected they would be working for the Major or Uncle John as she now called him, from time to time, even though he said he had retired but who knew for sure what that meant. Shelly suspected he would always have his finger in the pie, keeping his eye on things. He and Dolly would soon now live nearby. She had heard from Nancy who was still working as a fashion writer but she knew better, it was a good cover and could take her into a great many places. Archie her dearest friend would be married to his Caroline in the spring in London that would be a huge lavish affair to suit them and thrill Dolly, then a house in London too a wedding gift from Dolly.

Chapter 27

Spring had come early and after the wedding in London James and Shelly had returned home to their beloved and now peaceful Rosewood Hall. The cats and Toby had declared an uneasy truce. The geese had settled into their new home.

Shelly was sipping tea in the library waiting for James to come and join her, she was feeling very contented Spring was well and truly here and all the daffodils and tulips were out, she loved her husband and her home was safe, life was blissful she thought. James was happily working on the car Simon had started to build, he and Toby would come in soon, Jem had gone to call them in for tea, Mrs Barclay had made James's favourite fruit cake, all the staff could not do enough for him, he was kind and considerate to all, everything felt all was well with the world. They both loved the country life away from busy crowds content in each other's company she sighed blissfully. She heard James coming he was laughing, he walked in with a huge grin on his face, Toby was woofing happily too wagging his tail, she looked across at James as he said excitedly, "Guess what darling, I had finished some more of the work using the parts I had already got from the first crate, I wanted to see what other new parts were in the rest of the crates, so I could continue, they were tightly sealed and nailed down and they had been for a long time, it was heavy going to move and open them, I needed a crowbar to open them, inside I found all of parts of the car to complete it, I was very pleased to find them, they were all wrapped up in cloths, bound up like bandages in straw too, I pulled some out and then underneath I found this."

  He brought from behind his back an oily grubby looking oilskin sack tightly closed and after moving the tea tray out of the way he poured the contents of the sack onto the table, Shelly gasped, spilling out was a beautiful rainbow of colours made up of gold and sparkling precious stones.

The End.